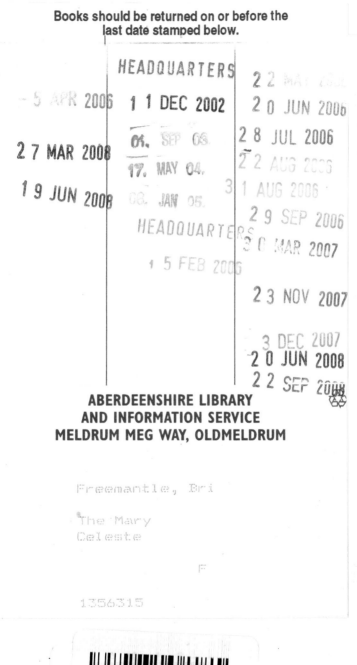

Books should be returned on or before the
last date stamped below.

HEADQUARTERS

- 5 APR 2006   1 1 DEC 2002   2 2 MAY

27 MAR 2008   01. SEP 03.   2 0 JUN 2006

19 JUN 2008   17. MAY 04.   2 8 JUL 2006

                 08. JAN 05.   2 2 AUG 2006

                                  3 1 AUG 2006

                 HEADQUARTERS   2 9 SEP 2006

                 1 5 FEB 2006   3 0 MAR 2007

                                  2 3 NOV 2007

                                  3 DEC 2007
                                  2 0 JUN 2008
                                  2 2 SEP 2008

ABERDEENSHIRE LIBRARY
AND INFORMATION SERVICE
MELDRUM MEG WAY, OLDMELDRUM

D0319663

Recent Titles by Brian Freemantle from Severn House

AT ANY PRICE
BETRAYALS
DIRTY WHITE
GOLD
THE KREMLIN CONSPIRACY
O'FARRELL'S LAW

THE MARY CELESTE

Brian Freemantle

This title first published in Great Britain 1999 by
SEVERN HOUSE PUBLISHERS LTD of
9–15 High Street, Sutton, Surrey SM1 1DF.
Originally published 1979 under the pseudonym *John Maxwell*.
This title first published in the U.S.A. 1999 by
SEVERN HOUSE PUBLISHERS INC of
595 Madison Avenue, New York, N.Y. 10022.

British Library Cataloguing in Publication Data

Freemantle, Brian
   The Mary Celeste
   1.   Mary Celeste (Ship) - Fiction
   2.   Suspense fiction
   I.   Title
   823.9'14 [F]

   ISBN 0 7278 5411 9

Printed and bound in Great Britain by
MPG Books Ltd, Bodmin, Cornwall.

*To John Killick, without
whose understanding so much
would have been impossible.
And to Rae, of course.*

'Wouldst thou' – so the helmsman answered –
'Learn the secrets of the sea?
Only those who brave its dangers
Comprehend its mystery.'

H. W. Longfellow, *The Secrets of the Sea*

Introduction

The *Mary Celeste*, an American half-brig of 282 tons, became a maritime legend a little past three o'clock on the afternoon of Wednesday, December 5, 1872.

Her precise location was latitude 38.20 N., by longitude 17.15 W., due east of the Azores and 591 miles from Gibraltar.

At that point, she passed a British brigantine, the *Dei Gratia*. By a coincidence – later to occur to many people as just too incredible – its master, Captain David Reed Morehouse, had been the dinner guest of the master of the *Mary Celeste*, Captain Benjamin Spooner Briggs, the night before the American vessel had sailed from New York with a cargo of 1,700 barrels of commercial alcohol, bound for Genoa.

Morehouse therefore knew the destination of the *Mary Celeste*. And recognised her to be on course, although sailing in the wrong direction. What he had first thought to be a fluttering distress signal was a ripped, tattered sail. The wheel, unmanned and unsecured, spun with every fresh thrust of wind.

Across the narrow gap separating them, Morehouse hailed his friend's ship. There was no response.

'What in God's name can have happened?' Morehouse asked first mate Oliver Deveau. The question has been posed repeatedly over the past hundred years in an attempt to solve the mystery of the world's most famous ghost ship.

Mutiny and murder was the attempted answer of Mr Frederick Solly Flood, Attorney-General and Admiralty Proctor of Gibraltar, the port to which a salvage crew from the *Dei Gratia* sailed the derelict. So convinced was the Attorney-General of crime – and that a chemical analyst had bungled an examination – that he suppressed for fourteen years a forensic report that stains on deck and upon a sword blade were not blood.

It was a conviction that caused him, within six weeks of the *Mary Celeste*'s being found, to write in an official report to the Board of Trade in London:

My own theory is that the crew got to the alcohol and in the fury of drunkenness murdered the master, whose name was Briggs, his wife and child and the chief mate; that they then damaged the bows of the vessel with the view of giving it the appearance of having struck on rocks or suffered a collision so as to induce the master of any vessel which might have picked them up, if they saw her at some distance, to think her not worth attempting to save; and that they did some time between the 25th of November (the date of the last log entry) and 5th December, escape on board some other vessel bound for some North or South American port or the West Indies.

The British government accepted his view. On March 11, 1873, Sir Edward Thornton, British Ambassador to Washington, passed on to the American administration evidence assembled in Gibraltar and asserted in his covering letter: 'You will perceive that the enquiries which have been initiated into the matter tend to rouse grave suspicion that the master and his wife and child were murdered by the crew.'

Responding to the British government's belief, U.S. Secretary to the Treasury William A. Richardson circularised customs officials throughout the United States on March 14, instructing them to look out for any ship carrying the alleged murderers to America.

Captain James Winchester, principal owner of the *Mary Celeste*, fled Gibraltar after giving evidence at an enquiry because he feared the official determination to prove a crime. To the U.S. Consul in Gibraltar, Horatio Jones Sprague, Captain Winchester wrote from the safety of New York on March 10, 1873, that he had quit the colony after being convinced by a friend there that the judge and Attorney-General intended arresting him for hiring the crew to murder their officers.

Captain Winchester wrote that although the supposition was ridiculous, 'From what you and everybody else in Gibraltar had told me about the Attorney-General, I did not know but he might do it as they seem to do just as they like'.

In such a fertile atmosphere of fear, suspicion and preconception – where innuendo became evidence and facts that didn't fit were blatantly concealed – the conjecture blossomed.

Four years before creating the legendary Sherlock Holmes, a Portsmouth doctor named Arthur Conan Doyle earned £30 for a short story purporting to be the account of a surviving passenger, J. Habakuk Jephson. Conan Doyle misnamed the derelict *Marie Celeste* and had J. Habakuk Jephson, 'the well known Brooklyn specialist on consumption', tell of another passenger, a half-caste from New Orleans named Septimus Goring, infiltrating the crew with henchmen, having the captain and officers killed and then sailing to Africa to establish a black empire there. Only a black stone shaped like a human ear, a talisman venerated by Negroes, saved J. Habakuk Jephson from death.

U.S. Consul Sprague sent the account – printed in the magazine *Cornhill* – to the State Department in Washington with the somewhat conservative verdict that it was 'replete with romance of a very unlikely or exaggerated nature'.

Amazingly, Attorney-General Flood seized it as an eye-witness account and informed the American authorities he was in contact with officials in Germany, believing that some of the *Mary Celeste*'s German crew were hiding there after joining Septimus Goring in the mutiny.

Mrs Fannie Richardson, wife of the *Mary Celeste*'s first mate Albert Richardson, told newspaper reporters on March 9, 1902, that she believed that her husband, the captain and the captain's wife and child had been murdered by the crew. Albert Richardson's sister, Mrs Priscilla Richardson Shelton, thought the same, while his brother, Captain Lyman Richardson, was convinced they had been killed by the crew of the *Dei Gratia*.

British author J. L. Hornibrook wrote in *Chamber's Journal* in 1904 that the crew were plucked from the ship, one by one, by 'a huge octopus or devil fish', recalling evidence at the enquiry of an axe-slash upon a deck-rail and suggested it had been caused in a futile attempt to fight the monster off.

The *Nautical Magazine* published an account by another alleged survivor of the vessel, in which Barbary pirates had boarded and slaughtered everyone aboard, and in the *British Journal of Astrology* in 1926 author Adam Bushey had the crew being 'dematerialised' because they had sailed at a psychically vital moment over the very spot where the lost city of Atlantis had sunk beneath the waves. Professor M. K. Jessup, instructor in Astronomy at Michigan University, wrote in a book, *UFO*, in 1955 that the people aboard the *Mary Celeste* didn't go downwards but upwards – snatched off the vessel by the crew of a hovering flying saucer.

As the theories became wilder, so did the 'facts' surrounding the finding of the *Mary Celeste* by the *Dei Gratia*.

Within half a century, it was unquestioningly believed that, when Captain Morehouse had come upon the vessel, there had been a half-eaten breakfast upon a cabin table, together with three cups of warm tea, a bottle of cough mixture open but unspilled upon another table, a phial of oil and a thimble beside a sewing machine upon which a child's dress was being repaired, the captain's watch still ticking, the stove in the galley warm to the touch, the galley fire burning, a cat peacefully asleep on a locker, sailors' pipes half-smoked, their washing hanging out to dry, the ship's boats still at their davits and no sign of damage or violence.

Not one of these suppositions is accurate.

There *were* facts established about the mystery. And upon them it is possible, I believe, for a conclusion to be suggested as to the fate of Captain Briggs, his wife Sarah, their two-year-old daughter Sophia and the seven-man crew.

Although fictionalised for ease of narrative, The '*Mary Celeste*' is based upon facts presented at the Gibraltar enquiry into the salvage claim by the *Dei Gratia* crew, and evidence taken from the surviving documents and statements of people directly involved in the affair.

On November 3, 1872, two days before the *Mary Celeste* slipped her moorings at Pier 50 on New York's East River, Captain Briggs wrote to his mother: 'Our vessel is in beautiful trim and I hope we shall have a fine passage.'

Despite fierce storms, it was so until November 25. At eight o'clock that morning, the half-brig was within six miles of Santa Maria, most easterly of the Azores group of islands, and in sight of Ponta Castello, its most easterly point.

Then disaster struck.

Four hours later, the *Mary Celeste* was a ghost ship.

Winchester, 1979   J.M.

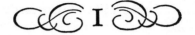

I

Already it had been officially recognised as the worst winter for centuries and the storms and gales that had scoured the Atlantic for months were even affecting Gibraltar. It was colder than normal for January and the familiar mist clung stubbornly to the Peak, like a tuft of sheep's wool on a hedgerow thistle.

Despite the coolness of the weathe., Attorney-General Frederick Solly Flood drove with the carriage hood down. He liked to be seen and his position within the tiny community to be marked with the respectful smiles and occasional head-nod of greeting, particularly since his additional appointment as Admiralty Proctor.

Speed was rarely possible anyway along the narrow, cluttered streets, but his coachman proceeded in the knowledge that there was no hurry.

Today the attention was greater than normal, because everyone knew where he was going. The *Gibraltar Chronicle and Commercial Intelligencer* had announced the commencement of the enquiry and even published a review of everything so far known about the American half-brig *Mary Celeste* since she had been brought in by the salvage crew.

Where the highway suddenly climbed, between the Fortress and the Governor's residence, he strained up, to catch sight of the tiny vessel far below in the bay, secure under its order of Admiralty arrest. Before he had finished with the witnesses who had been assembling during the past weeks, there would be available a great deal more information than that recorded by the *Intelligencer*. It wouldn't be easy, because Flood recognised that much effort had been devoted to destroying the evidence. But some still remained; more than the culprits suspected, he believed.

Upon that evidence he was going to prove that a dreadful crime had been committed. And the Board of Trade in London were going to appreciate the advantage of having as their representative a lawyer of his ability.

The far-away mist had merged with the rainclouds and as the carriage reached the Supreme Court building the shower began. There was already a crowd waiting for the doors to open and they began shifting impatiently at the prospect of being kept in the wet. The smiles of recognition were more obvious as the Attorney-General's carriage passed through the gate and pulled up in front. He saw among the spectators several foreign journalists, some even from as far away as New York, who had arrived to report the proceedings. He had already been interviewed by most of them and consented to having his picture taken to accompany the articles; he hoped they used the one of him in his official robes.

Flood responded to their greetings, remaining seated in the carriage until the door was opened for him. He hurried inside, a diminutive, portly man who held his head high in an effort to attain the height he didn't possess. He was aware but unworried that his critics called him 'pouter pigeon'. Some thought it an apt description; he had a jerky, bird-like habit of moving his head during conversations or court appearances and walked in abrupt, thrusting movements. Had he had any say in the appellation, Flood would have preferred being called a hawk. After all, a hawk was a wary, sharp-sighted bird. And that's how the enquiry was going to find him.

His clerk had already preceded him with his document case, so Flood went immediately to the robing room. He had almost finished dressing when the door tentatively opened behind him and Edward Baumgartner, the court registrar, entered.

'Morning, Attorney-General,' he said formally.

Flood nodded, but didn't speak.

'So at last everything is to become clear?'

Baumgartner spoke hopefully, anxious to convey the belief that the elucidation would come from the cleverness of Flood's questioning.

'That's my intention,' said Flood. He had been so long in Gibraltar that there was hardly a trace of his Irish accent. Only when he was excited or angry did it become pronounced.

'Quite a number of witnesses,' said Baumgartner.

'There's no hurry,' said the Attorney-General. 'I'll keep the court convened for a year if necessary.'

'Sure it won't be,' said Baumgartner, again intending the remark as admiration for the Attorney-General's ability to get to the truth. He waited, but when Flood failed to respond, said, 'Sir James would like to see you before we begin.'

Flood nodded again, as if he had anticipated the invitation, and followed the official out into the corridor and along to the Commissary's rooms.

Flood was glad it was Sir James Cochrane who was to preside at the hearing. Although it would have been an exaggeration for him to regard Sir James as a friend, the Attorney-General felt they understood each other. He was confident there would be no interference from Sir James if he extended the questioning beyond that which might have normally been regarded as necessary for the purpose of a salvage enquiry. With so little positive evidence, he was going to need such allowance. Would he succeed in obtaining a blurted confession? he wondered. They were probably simple men, even if they were criminals. It might be possible.

Sir James was at his window, staring out at the bay and Algeciras and La Linea beyond when Flood entered. He turned at the sound, smiling.

'A little madeira, for a cold day?' he asked.

'Thank you,' said Flood.

The judge poured from a decanter alongside the desk and then handed the Attorney-General his drink. 'Anticipating difficulties?' Sir James indicated the room beyond the closed door where the enquiry was assembling.

'If there's a guilty man there, he'll be evasive,' predicted Flood.

'*Is* there a guilty man?'

'There's been murder committed.'

'Murder!' The judge's astonishment showed in his voice.

'That's my belief.'

'It's a salvage claim we'll be considering,' said Sir James gently.

'Which makes the circumstances leading up to that salvaging very pertinent to the proceedings,' replied Flood.

'Quite,' said the judge. 'I'd just welcome a little more positive evidence than that which I've so far seen in the reports and affidavits. Murder's a strong accusation.'

'The evidence will be forthcoming.' Flood was confident. 'We've encountered a devilish clever scheme but I'm determined to upset the whole affair.'

'If there's been a crime, you'll get every support from me,' promised Sir James.

'I knew I would,' said Flood.

The judge finished his drink, replacing the glass on the decanter stand, and Flood took the lead to do the same. The man's assurance encouraged him.

'Consul Sprague tells me there's great interest in Washington over the whole affair,' said Sir James. 'I gather some well-known American journals have even sent special correspondents to report the enquiry.'

A look of irritation settled upon the Attorney-General's face.

'It's a pity the American Consul doesn't see fit to pursue his position here more rigorously,' he said.

It was accepted within the tiny British colony that there was antipathy between the two men but to Sir James it appeared that the Attorney-General's remark indicated more than their usual reserve towards each other.

'How so?' he said.

'He feels there might be a normal explanation for the affair,' disclosed Flood.

'Can't there be?'

'Not for anyone of average intelligence,' said Flood.

Sir James disguised the frown by returning to the window. The Attorney-General appeared very convinced of his case, he thought. He wondered if Flood had evidence of which he was unaware. London would expect him to do all he could to uncover a crime if one had been perpetrated; particularly murder.

Baumgartner appeared at the door, reminding them of the time. Sir James nodded, following the man from the room, with the Attorney-General behind him. In the corridor outside the enquiry chamber, Sir James paused to allow Flood to overtake and precede him, so that court protocol could be observed.

Everyone gazed at Flood as he bustled into the room. He

hurried expressionlessly to his place, turning to nod at the counsel representing the claimant captain and crew and the *Mary Celeste* owner only after he had shuffled through some papers, as if expecting some vital document to be missing.

Flood, who was fond of amateur dramatics, often thought of court and enquiry rooms as being very similar to the theatre, places where people staged performances. He gazed around the room, about which there was already an atmosphere of staleness because the windows were closed against the rain and cold, wondering at the portrayals they would witness before this hearing was concluded. He had no doubt that, whatever was attempted, he would be able to strip away the pretence.

From pre-hearing interviews and meetings, Flood was able to recognise everybody who would be testifying.

Captain James Winchester, the principal owner, who had travelled from New York to enter claim for possession of the vessel, sat immediately behind the counsels' table, a neat, precise man whose deeply tanned face indicated the mariner's life he had led before going ashore to become a businessman-sailor. It appeared to have been a successful transition. Winchester sat with a pince-nez upon his nose, pens regimented in his waistcoat pocket and an initialled briefcase by his side.

Respectfully in the row behind him and then assembled in order of priority were the crew of the *Dei Gratia*, shifting and moving in their uncertainty in such official surroundings, too ready to smile at whispered asides.

Nearest the aisle, as his seniority befitted, was Captain David Reed Morehouse, master of the *Dei Gratia*. He sat stiffly in his creased unaccustomed going-ashore suit, head positioned high by the starched collar, gazing straight ahead and refusing any involvement in the hushed conversation alongside. He was a formidable, almost wild-looking man, his beard grown freely over his chest and then parted, so that two bushy tails appeared to be growing from his chin.

Next to him sat Oliver Deveau, the first mate, who had transferred to the *Mary Celeste* and captained her to Gibraltar. He was a dark-haired, sallow-faced man in a thick serge suit. Like his commanding officer, he had a full, chest-length beard, but better combed than Morehouse's. The first mate's hair was greased tightly to his head and he kept darting looks at the captain, trying to emulate the man's demeanour.

Next to him was second mate John Wright and then seaman John Johnson, whom the Attorney-General knew to be the men who had crossed from the *Dei Gratia* in the ship's dory and had been the first to board the abandoned vessel. Then came seamen Charles Lund and Augustus Anderson, who, with Deveau, had formed the salvage crew. They wore reefer jackets and coarse work trousers. They sat rigidly, almost to attention, nervously alert for any summons they might receive.

The sort of people to be led into an incautious admission, decided Flood. They wouldn't expect him to have isolated a motive for the crime, any more than those who had led them into it.

The Attorney-General had already learned that the *Mary Celeste* was insured by the Atlantic Mutual Insurance Company of New York for $14,000, with her cargo covered through Lloyd's of London for £6,522. Not a fortune, Flood had to admit. But sufficient for desperate men to engage in some desperate activity. Upon established precedents, the *Dei Gratia* crew could anticipate an award of anything up to 40 per cent of that value if their claim were judged to be valid. For such men, it would be a lot of money.

In an aisle seat opposite the seamen was surveyor John Austin, who had carried out a comprehensive examination of the *Mary Celeste*, and further to the left, in his official place, was Thomas Vecchio, marshal of the court, who had impounded the vessel upon its arrival and accompanied Flood upon several personal visits.

To Flood's right sat Horatio Sprague. The American Consul smiled up at Flood's sudden attention. Sprague was a sparse, stooping man who was usually the listener in any conversation. He had a curiously attentive way of holding his head and he smiled a lot, an expression Flood frequently suspected to be one of mockery.

'All set, Frederick?'

Flood frowned at both the vernacular and the familiarity, particularly in surroundings where his title should have been most respected. Damned man had done it purposely, he thought.

18

Flood knew the American Consul had been a personal friend of the *Mary Celeste* captain and had even proposed him for the masonic lodge in Gibraltar. If anyone should have been seeking the real cause of the mystery, it was Sprague. Instead of which he kept attempting to curry favour with the Americans who had come to the colony for the enquiry. He was a disgrace to the office he was supposed to be holding, judged the Attorney-General.

'Of course I'm prepared,' he said.

'Gather there have been a lot of visits to the ship.'

'That's where the evidence is.'

'You've found some, then?'

Flood ignored the question, moving to the counsels' table. The Attorney-General was familiar with all the lawyers. Henry Pisani was representing Captain Morehouse and the crew in their claim for salvage and George Cornwell was entering Captain Winchester's formal claim for return of the vessel. Martin Stokes was appearing for the owners of the cargo. Flood thought them all to be dour, unimaginative men. If any inconsistency suddenly appeared in the evidence, he doubted whether any of these men would recognise it as such.

'Court will rise,' announced Baumgartner.

Flood was first on his feet as Sir James Cochrane entered and proceeded slowly to his place upon the raised dais. He nodded to the Attorney-General, the advocates and the American Consul before seating himself, immediately opening his file and a large, hard-bound note pad.

Everyone except Baumgartner resumed their seats. Taking up the official document lying ready before him, Baumgartner announced:

'This court, under the jurisdiction of Her Highness, Queen Victoria, is assembled to consider the demand for salvage entered by the master and crew of the British brigantine *Dei Gratia* against the owners and insurers of the *Mary Celeste*, the said vessel claimed to have been discovered derelict and abandoned on December 5, 1872, at latitude 38.20 N. by longitude 17.15 W., from which it was brought to this port.'

He sat down, half turning to the judge. Sir James cleared his throat, staring down into the well of the court.

'There has arisen over this matter much speculation and conjecture,' he said, choosing the advocates' bench as the object for his attention. 'It is therefore my intention to allow this enquiry to range as widely as I consider necessary to enable that speculation and conjecture to be resolved ... '

He paused at the obvious indication from the lawyer Cornwell that the man wished to speak.

'You have an observation?'

Cornwell rose, smiling gratefully:

'It is, of course, vital that everything considered necessary by this court is done to bring this investigation to a satisfactory conclusion. But I would respectfully remind the court that lying in the holds of the *Mary Celeste* is an extremely valuable cargo which the owners are still under contract to deliver to Genoa ... '

'What is your point, Mr Cornwell?'

'That the vessel should be released from Admiralty seizure and restored to Captain Winchester as soon as possible to enable that contract to be fulfilled,' said Cornwell.

Cochrane lowered his head over his papers and Flood recognised the indication of annoyance. It was several moments before Cochrane looked up.

'I am aware of the contractual obligations binding Captain Winchester and his associates,' he said evenly. 'I am even more aware of the obligations under which this court has been brought into session and which I, as a judge appointed by Her Majesty, the Queen of England, am required to fulfil. This enquiry will continue as long as I deem it necessary. And the vessel in question will remain under Admiralty bond until I decide it shall be released.'

Cornwell hesitated for a moment, then slowly sat down. His 'Of course, sir,' was barely audible.

As Cornwell sat, Cochrane looked over to the Attorney-General. There was no expression on the judge's face, but Flood knew the reason for the look. He was as intrigued as Sir James at the request for speed before an enquiry had even commenced. Since the arrival of the *Mary Celeste* on December 12, barely a day had passed when something had not arisen to provide fresh grounds for suspicion. He glanced sideways at the American Consul.

It was remarkable that he appeared to be the only one who recognised it, thought Flood. But now the enquiry was about to begin.

It would not take long for them to realise how obtuse they had all been.

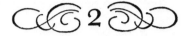

2

Benjamin Briggs had been schooled to conceal pride; certainly in any material achievement or possession.

'Thy money perish with thee,' he murmured, remembering. An Act of the Apostles. One of his father's favourites. His father-in-law's, too, by strange coincidence. From his wife's father, it was understandable. Expected, even. The man was a clergyman, after all.

His own father's devoutness to the Scriptures had surprised Benjamin in his early youth, before he had sailed under the man's rigid captaincy and come to realise how easy it was to feel the power of God at sea.

His father had been a good teacher, of Scriptures as well as seamanship. A strict man; spartan, by some assessments. But always fair, as Benjamin knew he himself was fair to his men, not by conscious, thinking effort, as if attempting to emulate his father, but naturally because he was imbued with the quality so that he knew no other way to behave.

That was why he felt embarrassment at the realisation of his pride, because he knew his father would have criticised it. He trailed his hand along the top-gallant rail, savouring the texture of the fresh varnish and the new woodwork beneath. Perhaps, on this occasion, the man would have understood. Maybe felt the sensation himself; he had sufficient cause to be proud, after all. Four sons, each a ship's captain, carrying on the family tradition. And his only daughter married to one.

Now, reflected Briggs, he was even more than a captain. At thirty-seven years of age, part-owner, too. Admittedly only a third share, but enough. Particularly in a newly rebuilt vessel like the *Mary Celeste,* trim and clean from stem to stern.

'She's a beautiful ship, Benjamin.'

Briggs hurriedly pulled his hand away at the sound of his wife's voice, as if he had been discovered doing something wrong, and turned, smiling, to her.

'I was just thinking so myself.'

'I know.'

'Is it obvious?' he asked.

She smiled at the concern in his voice. 'Why ever shouldn't it be?' she said.

'Hardly seemly.'

'What's unseemly about appreciating one's achievements?'

'False pride,' he suggested.

'Where's the falsity?' she demanded. 'You've every reason for pride. There's a difference between that and conceit, surely?'

'You think it was the right decision, then?'

She shook her head, the irritation taking the smile from her face even though she knew the reason for his doubt. Until Benjamin's decision to buy a share in the *Mary Celeste,* she had not fully realised how deeply he had been affected by his father's near-bankruptcy after the business venture in Wareham, Massachusetts, had failed.

'You know how I feel about it,' she said. 'It was a wise and sensible thing to do. We decided that.'

'Even though it's taken so much of our money that we have to think before taking private horse carriages to visit friends here in New York?'

She sighed. Because of the horse disease, the horse-cars were not running on the east side of the city and they had been able to make only one excursion into Central Park with Sophia, when Sarah's clergyman brother William had paid the $10 for the vehicle to come to collect them.

'Stop remembering your father's failure,' she said. 'He put his money into a shore venture. You're putting yours into what you know best, the sea.'

She tiptoed, to raise her face to his, kissing him lightly. 'And if it hadn't happened, we probably wouldn't have married.'

It was a long-established family joke that they had been childhood sweethearts and certainly for as long as she could remember Benjamin had been part of her life. She could still recall his arrival at the age of five, with his near-penniless mother, to live with her pastor father at the manse at Marion. It had been four years before his father had recovered sufficient money to buy a cottage of their own. And then Sippican had been only a mile from Marion, so they continued to see each other every day. All that time, she thought fondly. And never once a moment of boredom or unhappiness with the man. She considered herself a fortunate woman.

He kissed her back.

'And that would have been the tragedy of my life,' he said seriously.

'So let's count our blessings, not doubt them.'

'That's what I was doing,' said Briggs.

'After this voyage,' she said, business-like, nodding towards the quayside from which the cargo was being swung into the holds, 'we will have gone a long way towards recovering our investment and repaying our loans. We know there's a return cargo in Messina. Within the year, we could be showing a profit. Don't fret so.'

Briggs smiled at her encouragement. Sometimes, in his prayers, he thanked God for guiding him to a woman like Sarah. Slight, even giving the misleading impression of being frail, the skin of her face glowing as it always did after her morning toilet and the regulation one hundred splashes of ice-cold water against her cheeks, shown now to its best and healthy advantage by the severe way she had of dressing her hair, parted in the middle and combed straight back from her forehead and gathered into a tight knot beneath the bonnet. A beautiful woman, he decided. And more. No man could have sought a better mother for Arthur or Sophia. Nor a wiser housekeeper for their affairs. When the opportunity had arisen to buy a third share in the *Mary Celeste* it had been Sarah who itemised immediately the state of their finances, made the calculations about the loan they would have to raise and then presented him with an account record so that he could assess whether they could afford it.

Briggs realised that she was as much a companion as a wife, a special friend to whom he could always turn and from whom he would always receive the correct advice.

He recognised suddenly the reason for the completeness of the pride he had experienced earlier at the top-gallant rail. Perhaps the sensation had not even been pride. Rather, it had been the satisfaction of knowing that the purchase of the vessel had filled the one vacuum in an otherwise perfect life. He had a perfect wife and a perfect family and a perfect career and now he was a man of substance, an owner-captain. Part-owner, he thought again. But hardly a qualification. Definitely not one that Captain Winchester, the principal shareholder, was invoking.

'Your ship', the man had said during their dinner the previous night. And meant it, Briggs knew. He decided he liked Captain Winchester. A blunt speaker, almost to the point of curtness. But a no-nonsense man, the sort of person with whom Briggs preferred to deal. He had left every encounter with Winchester knowing exactly where he stood, without any half-doubts about anything the man might have intended but held back from conveying in case there were need to alter his opinion at some later stage. And about that he was lucky, he knew, thinking back to involvements with other shipping men.

A man who noticed details, Briggs attached importance to Winchester's action when the man had learned that he intended taking Sarah and Sophia on the voyage to Genoa. By noon the following day, a second boat had arrived to supplement the longboat already aboard.

'Hardly necessary on a ship as sound as this,' Winchester had said. 'Just regarded it as a sensible precaution.'

It had shown a consideration far beyond that which Briggs would have expected most owners to show, even though the man must have known from the care he was taking with the selection of the crew that Briggs was fully aware of the added responsibility of being accompanied by all but one of his family.

As if in reminder, Sophia's close-curled golden head jerked over the lip of the companion-way she was noisily insisting upon clambering up herself, without the assistance of the cook-steward who followed.

Sarah went immediately to the child, looking beyond her into the galley area.

'Sorry you were bothered, Mr Head,' she apologised.

'No bother, ma'am,' said the man.

Sarah returned, the baby cupped in the crook of her arm. The child leaned away from its mother, reaching for the rail from which she could watch the activity on the quayside below.

'Before this voyage is over, there's a risk of her becoming spoiled by the crew,' said Sarah. 'They all seem to love her.'

'Pity Arthur can't come as well,' said Briggs.

'At seven, his need is for schooling,' replied Sarah immediately.

'I'll still miss him.'

'No more than I. But were you allowed to sacrifice lessons to sail with your father?'

'No.'

'Then neither will Arthur be permitted.'

'He'll not be permitted much,' predicted Briggs. During the voyage, their son was to live with his grandmother; Briggs knew the boy would receive the same strict discipline he and his brothers had been given.

To ease the child's weight, Sarah lifted Sophia up on to the top of the rail, standing with her arms protectively around her.

Briggs patted a supporting stanchion reflectively.

'Pity there aren't bulwarks,' he said.

'What?'

'Proper bulwarks,' repeated Briggs. 'If a sea runs, these open rails can be dangerous for an experienced seaman, let alone a woman and a two-year-old child.'

'If it's too bad, we can stay in the cabin, as I have before,' said Sarah. 'And when we're at sea, we'll have Sophia on a safety line whenever she's on deck.'

Briggs nodded at the recollection of his wife's previous trips with him. Ten years before they had spent their honeymoon on a Mediterranean voyage, when he had commanded the schooner *Forest King*. She had enjoyed it so much that there had been other voyages during his captaincy of the *Arthur* and the *Sea Foam*. There was no danger in having a woman like Sarah aboard ship; rather, it was almost like having an extra crew member.

'I must work,' he said, excusing himself and moving forward to where the chief mate was supervising the loading.

Briggs felt the greatest satisfaction at the crew he had assembled, at signing Albert Richardson as first mate. They had sailed together before and Richardson was as complete a seaman as any

27

Briggs had ever encountered: indeed, he had been surprised that Richardson had taken the voyage, qualified as he now was to be master of his own vessel. Briggs regarded it as a compliment, aware without conceit that Richardson thought of him as a good master and seaman and saw the trip as a qualification voyage, the last he would undergo before applying for his own command. And that was in little doubt, newly married as he was to Captain Winchester's niece, Frances Spates.

Nearer the cargo, Briggs could detect the odour of the commercial alcohol and brought his hand to his face in an instinctive gesture of revulsion.

Richardson smiled at the movement.

'Stinks right enough, sir,' he said.

'Going well, Mr Richardson?'

'We'll be completed on time tomorrow,' the first mate assured him.

'Any problems?'

'Certainly not in stowage.'

'What then?' asked Briggs, detecting the reservation in the man's voice.

Richardson walked nearer the hoists, taking the captain with him, and gestured down into the hold.

'Red oak barrels,' identified Richardson. 'Leaky stuff.'

'We'll have to be mindful of the danger,' agreed Briggs.

'Bad time of the year for weather,' Richardson reminded him. 'And there have been storms enough as it is.'

'I'd considered as southerly a course as possible.'

'Probably best.'

'How much inboard?' Briggs gestured into the hold.

'One thousand, three hundred barrels,' said Richardson, consulting the consignment board in his hand.

'Another four hundred to come, then,' said Briggs. 'What about the ballast figure?'

'Thirty tons of stone.'

'Should be sufficient,' said Briggs. He indicated the fo'c'sle: 'What about the crew?'

'Fine lot,' judged Richardson. 'We'll have no trouble there.'

'My thinking, too,' said Briggs, pleased at the other man's assessment.

28

'I gather that the German, Arien Martens, is a qualified mate.'

'Seems like we'll have a very expert crew,' said Briggs.

Richardson obviously appreciated the reference to his recently obtained master's ticket.

'Then it should be an easy voyage,' he said.

'One of the easiest I've undertaken, I hope,' said Briggs. He moved away from the hold, towards the companion-way leading to the quayside. 'I've to go ashore,' he said, passing over command. 'I'm minded it will take me about three hours.'

Because he was on official business and would therefore be reimbursed for the expense, Briggs had ordered a private carriage. Despite the ban on horse-cars, the streets of the city still shifted and heaved with movement; perhaps it was because there were so many immigrants, but Briggs always felt that, instead of being just one port, New York was a mixture of all he had ever visited, a kaleidoscope of cultures and sounds and accents.

To some, he knew, it was confusing, but Briggs always considered it exciting and vibrant, just like the whole land was now that the war was over. Increasingly, since the armistice and from the evidence he had seen from the American ports he visited, comparing them and their business efficiency against those he knew from foreign jetties, Briggs had determined that America would grow into an important country. And he would be a part of that growth. He relaxed easily against the worn leather of the seat, gazing out at the jostled, thronged streets and experiencing again the satisfaction that had first come at the rail of the *Mary Celeste*. There could be few people in this city or even this country as fortunate as he. Consciously he controlled the emotion, annoyed with himself for permitting it a second time. He'd make the opportunity before the *Mary Celeste* sailed to visit a church and thank God for his blessings.

They were expecting him at the offices of the United States Shipping Commissioner and the documents were ready. He signed first the articles of agreement, then the list of persons comprising the crew. Within fifteen minutes he was back in the carriage, heading for the offices of J. W. Winchester & Co.

The principal owner was waiting for him, too.

'We've obtained cargo insurance from the Atlantic Mutual covering the freight,' announced Winchester, after they had shaken hands and Winchester had shown Briggs to a chair bordering his desk. 'Total of $3,400.'

'What premium?' asked Briggs. Commercial alcohol was a more difficult freight than some.

'Two and a half.'

'Reasonable enough,' said Briggs.

'How's loading?'

'Almost complete,' said Briggs. 'I'd like to thank you again, incidentally, for that second boat.'

Winchester shrugged dismissively:

'Still stormy in the Atlantic, by all accounts.'

'I've delayed getting a forecast until nearer the sailing,' said Briggs.

Winchester glanced across at the barometer which hung against the far wall.

'The glass is far enough down even here,' he said. 'God knows what it'll be like out at sea.'

'Sarah is a good sailor,' said Briggs confidently.

'What about the young one?'

'We'll have to wait and see.'

'Still happy with the ship?'

'It would be difficult to be otherwise,' said Briggs. 'She's a fine vessel.'

'You still haven't sailed her yet,' Winchester reminded him.

'Captain Spates was complimentary enough,' said Briggs. Spates had been the captain for the vessel's previous voyage, from Puerto Rico.

'And he's an experienced enough man,' conceded Winchester. He went to a cabinet against the wall and returned with a bottle and two glasses. 'A toast to the voyage,' he suggested.

Briggs raised his hand, in a halting movement.

'I mean no offence,' he said, 'but I don't take alcohol.'

Winchester paused, looking up at his new captain and business partner.

'Not ever?' he asked, remembering the previous night's refusal at dinner.

'Never.'

The man set the bottle down, whisky in only one glass. 'Then it'll be a solitary toast,' he said, raising his glass. 'To our partnership and to the successful voyage of the *Mary Celeste*.'

'I'll accept the sentiment, if not the drink,' said Briggs.

When Briggs returned to the *Mary Celeste* two hours later, Richardson was waiting for him. During the final loading of the day, the block had slipped, dropping the hoist suddenly. A barrel iron had caught the regular lifeboat, which had been brought from the stern davits on to the deck for the caulking to be checked. The planking had been stoved in for about three feet on the port side, near the stem.

'We'll not be able to get that repaired on time,' said Briggs immediately.

'What about a replacement?' asked Richardson. He had been quietened by the incident, regarding it as his fault for attempting two jobs at the same time.

'I'll speak to Captain Winchester first thing in the morning,' promised Briggs. He looked back to the main hatch, over which the second boat Winchester had provided was to be secured on fenders.

'That might come in handier than we first thought,' he said.

'Smaller than this, though,' pointed out Richardson.

'Aye,' agreed Briggs. 'A proper replacement would obviously be better ... ' He paused. 'Checked the rafts, just in case another longboat isn't available?'

'Yes,' said Richardson. 'They're brand new.'

Briggs smiled gratefully at his first mate's professionalism.

'If we can't get another longboat, then with what we've already been given by Captain Winchester and with the rafts, we'll still be able to sail on schedule,' he said.

'Right enough,' accepted Richardson. 'We're more than adequately covered on safety regulations.'

Briggs straightened from the damaged longboat, gazing down at the splintered hole. It was beyond repair.

'Still annoying, though,' he said.

'Yes,' said Richardson. 'Damned annoying.'

He registered the grimace from Briggs and remembered too late the captain's dislike of bad language, even without his wife aboard.

Briggs was immediately aware of the other man's discomfort and moved to cover it.

'There were times,' he said, 'when something like this would have been regarded as a bad omen.'

Richardson sighed, content that he hadn't caused any offence. 'Not with the crew we've got aboard,' he said confidently.

As he moved towards his cabin, Briggs heard the sounds of the melodeon Sarah had brought aboard to accompany her singing. She played as well as she sang, he thought fondly, pausing outside the cabin to listen to the hymn.

He turned, staring back up the companion-way and towards the unseen lifeboat. It was an irritation, he decided. But nothing more. Nevertheless, he would sail happier if he could obtain a replacement.

3

The Attorney-General sat at his bench, his head lowered, seemingly more interested in the documents before him than in what Captain Winchester was saying. His manner obviously more respectful since his rebuff from the judge, Cornwell had taken his client easily through the formal evidence necessary to enter claim for the vessel and Flood had watched while the New York shipowner had grown more relaxed and confident in the legal surroundings.

Which was exactly how Flood wanted the man: relaxed and confident and completely unsuspecting.

Flood, looking up in apparent surprise when Cornwell muttered his thanks to the witness and sat down, gave the appearance of unreadiness when invited by Cochrane to ask questions, fumbling through the papers on the table. When he finally rose, Winchester was smiling indulgently, imagining incompetence. Flood determined it would not be a smile to last for long.

'So the *Mary Celeste* had been rebuilt?' he said, taking Winchester back to the very beginning of his evidence.

The owner nodded. 'In 1868 or thereabouts. She had originally been constructed in Nova Scotia with only one deck. But she was wrecked and then rebuilt to have two decks, her length extended to 103 feet and her size brought up to 282 tons.'

'A new vessel, in fact?'

'Virtually so, yes.'

'A valuable ship?'

Winchester hesitated, frowning. 'Yes,' he agreed finally.

Flood sorted through some papers in front of him.

'Insured, I understand, for some $14,000?'

'Yes,' said Winchester again.

'And the present cargo covered by the owners on the London market for some £6,500?'

Again Winchester paused before agreeing, shortly: 'Yes.'

'In addition to which there was your freight insurance of $3,400?'

'Yes.' The repetition came almost in a sigh.

Winchester was patronising him, Flood recognised. Which was how he wanted it to be.

'When did you acquire her?'

'With a consortium of other men, in October 1869.'

'Captain Briggs formed part of that consortium?'

'Not the original group. He purchased his interest in October last year.'

'Just prior to sailing, in fact?'

'Yes.'

'You knew him well?'

'At first, only by reputation. And that was of an above-average captain. When he joined my company, I came to believe that reputation well founded. I was proud to have him as a partner.'

'Describe him.'

'A first-class master and navigator,' said Winchester immediately. 'I regarded him as an asset to the company.'

'A first-class master and navigator,' repeated Flood slowly. 'Yet he was to be parted from a ship in which he had so recently purchased part-ownership on his very first voyage.'

Winchester appeared uncertain. 'Excuse me, sir,' he said, 'but I don't understand if that's a question.'

'Not a question, Captain Winchester,' said Flood. 'More an observation from which a question can be formulated. What would induce a man of Captain Brigg's ability and experience, accompanied by his wife and child, to abandon ship without any apparent reason?'

'That is a question to which I have devoted a great deal of consideration —' began Winchester, but Flood interrupted, wanting to tilt the man's composure slightly.

' — then give us the benefit of that consideration, Captain Winchester.'

'I have come to no rational, logical conclusion,' said Winchester, unruffled by the Attorney-General.

'Sea monsters, perhaps?' said Flood, anticipating the outburst of laughter and the annoyance it would cause Winchester.

'It must have been something quite frightening and quite unexpected. It's been a stormy season and I can only assume it was some manifestation of weather that we shall never know.'

'You've described Captain Briggs as a first-class captain?'

'Yes.'

'The sort of man to panic?'

'Definitely not.'

Winchester was unsettled now, thought Flood. The questioning was proceeding exactly as he had intended.

'But wouldn't it indicate panic of the most hysterical kind to abandon with sails apparently set an obviously seaworthy, utterly sound vessel through some manifestation of the weather and commit himself, his family and his crew to a smaller, less seaworthy, less sound lifeboat?'

Winchester did not respond.

'Wouldn't it?' insisted the Attorney-General.

'That could be an interpretation,' admitted Winchester reluctantly.

'The only interpretation?' pressed Flood.

'I suppose so.'

'Yet Captain Briggs was an experienced, first-class mariner unlikely to panic whatever the circumstances.'

'That is my belief,' said Winchester.

'Then if that's the case, your theory about the weather cannot be valid, can it?'

'Before going ashore to run my company I spent many years at sea,' said Winchester. 'There can arise upon an ocean freak conditions the like of which no man who is not a sailor can ever imagine ... conditions that would cause the unlikeliest reaction from the most experienced master.'

'Are you inviting this enquiry to believe that somewhere near the Azores group of islands there was such a bizarre occurrence ... so bizarre that a sane man committed his wife and baby to the perils of a lifeboat ... '

'I don't ask this enquiry to be persuaded into any conclusion,' said Winchester. 'I am merely trying to assist in answering your questions to the best of my ability.'

The Attorney-General allowed the surprise to register at the defiance, the silence building up for effect. Finally he said: 'Surely you are willing to persuade the court into one conclusion?'

'Again I lose your drift, sir,' protested Winchester.

'You have not, if my recollection of your evidence-in-chief is correct, disputed the fact that the *Mary Celeste* was found abandoned?'

'But how can I?' said Winchester.

Ignoring the question, Flood continued: 'And therefore you do not oppose the salvage claim?'

Winchester looked towards Captain Morehouse in the well of the court, then towards the judge, as if seeking guidance.

'Can you see any reason why salvage should not be granted to those making the claim before this enquiry today?' persisted the Attorney-General.

'I am not conducting this enquiry,' said Winchester adroitly. 'That is a decision for the judge, after considering all of the evidence.'

The Attorney-General concealed completely his annoyance at the other man's avoidance of the question. He had imagined he had sufficiently unsettled Captain Winchester to make him blurt out some unconsidered denial, from which he could have moved further to dislodge the man.

'Were you aware that Captain Briggs sailed armed?' he suddenly demanded.

'Armed?' echoed Winchester, face open with astonishment.

'A sword was found concealed beneath the bunk of his cabin,' said Flood. He hesitated, reaching beneath a cloth covering the exhibits and held it up. 'This sword,' he announced.

Winchester smiled, patronising again. 'A souvenir from some earlier voyage, surely?' he said, looking out into the court at the scattered sound of amusement.

'The thought amuses you, Captain Winchester?'

'The thought of Captain Briggs arming himself with a cutlass amuses me,' said the owner.

'I do not consider this a cutlass.'

'Forgive me, sir,' said Winchester, more openly patronising. 'A sword of any kind.'

Flood became aware of Cochrane's attention upon him and

36

realised that the judge imagined he had lost control of the questioning.

'Would your amusement remain if I told you that there was evidence of that sword being hastily wiped to do away with the traces of blood which stained the blade?' he demanded.

The attitude of condescension fell away from the witness. Winchester became immediately serious, looking towards the lawyer representing him and then back to Flood.

'Of course I would not be amused,' he said. 'I know nothing of any bloodstains.'

'There were more upon the decking,' continued Flood. 'Tell me, Captain Winchester, what freak weather conditions put bloodstains upon sword blades and ships' decking?'

Winchester shrugged, but did not reply.

'Do you persist in your view that the weather is the root of this apparent tragedy?' said Flood.

'I was trying to assist the enquiry,' repeated Winchester irritably. 'I was not insisting that it *was* the weather. How can I? No one will ever know.'

'Perhaps we might come to learn the truth,' Flood said quickly. 'This enquiry has hardly begun, after all.'

He went back to his papers, seeking nothing but wanting a pause for the remark to be assimilated by everyone in the room.

'Was Captain Briggs an abstemious man?' he asked.

'A teetotaller,' replied Winchester.

'And the crew?'

'I know the first mate, Richardson, to be a non-drinker,' said the owner.

'How so?'

'He was recently married to a relation of mine, a niece.'

'And the remainder of the crew?'

'Predominantly German,' said Winchester. 'There was no indication of any drunkenness among them prior to the sailing. Captain Briggs went to particular trouble to ensure he had as good a crew as he could muster and before he sailed he expressed himself well pleased with the men he'd got.'

'Remind the enquiry of the cargo of the *Mary Celeste*,' said the Attorney-General.

'Commercial alcohol,' said Winchester.

'Surprised as you were to learn there had been found a blood-stained sword aboard, how surprised would you be to be told that there is evidence of that cargo being broached?'

'Broached?'

'That was my word, sir,' said Flood.

'Which in shipping circles has a rather definite meaning,' said Winchester, refusing to be subjugated by the confident little man before him. 'Are you telling me that there is evidence of the cargo being tampered with ... pierced, in fact, for the liquid to be drawn off?'

Winchester was proving a more difficult witness than he had imagined he would be, decided Flood. A man of surprising composure, in fact. Unless, of course, he had anticipated the awkwardness of the questioning.

'To my certain knowledge, there are three barrels in the hold of that vessel lying out there ... ' said the Attorney-General, gesturing towards the window and the bay beyond, '... completely empty of their contents.'

'Were the sides pierced? Or the barrel heads removed?' demanded Winchester.

'The barrels were empty,' reiterated Flood, uncomfortable at the man's insistence upon a method. 'How do you imagine that came about?'

'A hypothesis again,' said Winchester. 'But by its very nature, alcohol is inclined towards evaporation.'

'If three barrels were to evaporate, then wouldn't the tendency be for the whole cargo to diminish?'

'I'm not a scientist,' said Winchester. 'I don't know the answer to that.'

Shadows began to lengthen in the enquiry chamber and Flood became aware of Cochrane shifting at his bench. It would not be long before the judge brought the proceedings to a close, realised the Attorney-General. It was time finally to shake this complacent man.

'Isn't there a far more sinister interpretation to be drawn from the inexplicable disappearance of a sober, experienced sailor and his family from a sound vessel with its sails set than some nebulous conjecture about freak weather and alcohol evaporation?' he demanded, allowing the aggression to show.

38

Again Winchester looked from his lawyer to Cochrane and Flood felt the stirrings of satisfaction, aware of the man's concern.

' ... I don't know ... ' attempted Winchester, but the Attorney-General overrode him.

' ... with barrels of alcohol empty and bloodstained swords lying beneath cabin bunks, isn't a far more likely explanation for this tragedy an orgy of drunkenness on the part of the crew, who then put to a death most foul their captain, his family and perhaps even the next most senior officers?'

Winchester made an unknowing movement with his shoulders, his bewilderment obvious.

'But to what point ... what motive?' he said uncertainly.

'Can't you help us with that, Captain Winchester?'

Flood purposely kept his voice low, wanting it to carry no farther than Cochrane and the witness, so that the uncertainty of the crewmen of the *Dei Gratia* still to give evidence would be heightened.

Captain Winchester stared directly across the short distance separating him from the Attorney-General, straightening in a positive effort to recover himself. Flood thought it might have been an illusion in the failing light, but he got a fleeting impression that the man's deeply tanned face had suddenly lightened in colour.

'I want an explanation of that remark, sir,' he said, his voice almost as quiet as Flood's.

'My function at this enquiry isn't to provide explanations,' said Flood, aware that his arrogance would annoy the other man. 'It is to seek them out. Tell me, Captain Winchester, why it was felt necessary even before the commencement of this enquiry for your counsel to urge haste for the release of the *Mary Celeste*?'

The man's face *had* paled, decided the Attorney-General. He wondered whether the cause were anger or fear.

'As Mr Cornwell explained,' said Winchester stiffly, 'there is lying in the holds of the *Mary Celeste* a valuable cargo which my company is contracted to deliver upon a certain date. While my clients are prepared to make certain allowances for the circumstances surrounding the vessel, they seek discharge as soon as possible. There is also a perishable cargo awaiting shipment from Messina.'

'Delivery of the alcohol for the full, agreed payment?'

There was no complacency now about Captain Winchester. He looked warily across the enquiry room, forehead lined in an attempt to follow the Attorney-General's questioning.

'Of course,' he said finally.

'Nearly $37,000?'

'Slightly less than that.'

'If we add to that value the value of the ship, some $14,000, we have an aggregate of about $51,000?'

There was a sudden movement to the Attorney-General's left and the lawyer Cornwell rose.

'For some time,' he said to the judge, 'I have been anticipating some intervention on your behalf at the worrying direction of my learned friend's questions. As this has not been forthcoming, I seek an assurance from the Attorney-General, through you, that there is some point or purpose to this somewhat bizarre interrogation, reminding the court at the same time that these are civil proceedings into a claim for salvage, nothing more.'

Cochrane jerked up at the impudence of the interruption. 'Are you questioning my conduct of this enquiry, sir?' he demanded.

'Under no circumstances,' said Cornwell instantly, less abashed than he had been during his earlier clash with the man. 'It is Mr Flood's conduct I am calling into doubt.'

With an obvious effort, Cochrane controlled his anger. His voice almost unnaturally level, he said, 'I made it quite clear at the commencement of this enquiry, Mr Cornwell, that I intended to allow as much investigation as I deemed necessary to get to the heart of this matter. In my opinion, there has been nothing about the Attorney-General's behaviour to earn the reminder from me of the nature of this hearing, any more than I need such remonstrances from you ... ' He paused, turning to Flood. 'And I leave it to the Attorney-General to provide what assurances he feels necessary about the point or purpose of his questioning.'

Rejected again, Cornwell sat down and Flood turned to him, happy at the further confusion the man's interruption had created.

'I am delighted to assure my learned friend that every question I have posed today and will pose during future days has a very real and definite purpose ... the purpose of finding the correct solution to this affair ... '

He turned back to where Captain Winchester was shifting at his place. The man was greatly disconcerted, decided Flood.

'You are familiar with salvage claims?' he asked.

'No,' said the owner. 'Fortunately they have been rare occurrences in my experience.'

'I'm sure the court is delighted to learn of your admirable record,' said Flood. 'But you will be aware, of course, of the nature of awards ... the percentages normally allocated by courts?'

'I understand they vary.'

'Indeed they do, depending upon the circumstances and the enquiry's acceptance of the evidence produced before it. But tell me, Captain Winchester, what would you expect a court to award in this case if it were satisfied that the claim from the crew of the *Dei Gratia* were completely justified?'

Winchester took a long time to reply, twice looking to his counsel as if he expected a fresh challenge.

At last he said, 'From loosely established precedents, I would assume them to be looking towards something around 50 per cent of the total of cargo and ship value.'

'Which we have already agreed is around $50,000. So we are talking of a sum around $25,000?'

'I suppose so.'

'A fair sum of money?'

'Yes.'

'Particularly when, with the exception of a few barrels, the cargo remains intact and ready to be unloaded at Genoa whenever the *Mary Celeste* is released. For full and complete settlement of some further $37,000 on top of any salvage award?'

Again Winchester looked to his counsel, but when the man remained seated he came back to the Attorney-General and said, 'I am at a loss to understand the point of this discussion.'

'Are you, Captain Winchester?'

'What inference are you making, sir!' demanded the owner.

'Raising questions again,' said Flood easily. 'Questions to which I shall return during the course of this enquiry until we get what I consider are satisfactory answers ... '

He turned from the witness, towards Cochrane, estimating this to be the precise moment he should stop, to cause the maximum effect.

'That concludes my questioning for today,' he said. 'But I would seek to lodge in the court's record the request to recall this witness during the course of the hearing if it is considered necessary.'

'The court notes your request,' said Cochrane, rising gratefully. 'The court will be adjourned until tomorrow.'

The moment the judge left the chamber, Winchester hurried towards his counsel, gesturing as he did so for the American Consul to accompany him.

Flood smiled, well satisfied with his first day. He took time collecting his scattered documents and then walked from the room, aware that they would have seen his expression and found it as unsettling as they had his cross-examination. He had just disrobed when Baumgartner appeared at the door.

'Sir James would like to see you,' he said.

'Went well today,' said the registrar, as they walked towards the judge's chambers. It was more of a question than an observation.

'It will get better as the days progress,' predicted Flood confidently.

Cochrane was at the window, as he had been during their encounter before the enquiry had begun, when the Attorney-General entered.

'Thank you for your support,' he said immediately, to Cochrane.

'Gave you the undertaking before the proceedings began,' the other man replied. 'You raised a lot of questions in there today.'

'And I intend getting the answers,' said Flood.

'You think Winchester is involved in whatever happened?'

'He was too composed ... unworried. Should have been far more outraged by the obvious inferences I was making.'

'He could just be a dour man,' pointed out the judge.

'More likely a guilty one.'

'I'll need more than innuendo and suspicion.'

'You'll have your evidence,' said Flood. 'I'm *determined* you'll have your evidence.'

He glanced at the carriage clock upon the mantelpiece of the judge's chambers. By now, he decided, Dr Patron would be well into his analyses. Of all the evidence, that which Dr Patron was going to produce would be the most damning.

Because it was the nearest place available, they went to the house of the American Consul, Horatio Sprague. Cornwell sat at the desk, jotting pad before him, with Pisani opposite, but Captain Winchester, engulfed by anger, was unable to sit. Instead he strode about the room, jerking his arms out for emphasis, a vein pumping in his forehead. Sprague lapsed into his customary role of listener.

'Railroaded,' protested Winchester. 'The damned man has got a conviction about murder and is determined to railroad me into some position of guilt, the instigator of a crime with God knows who.'

'I've rarely been present at judicial proceedings like it,' said Cornwell, more controlled.

'I'm not for a moment suggesting that you are in any way involved,' Sprague said to the ship-owner, 'but broached cargo and bloodstained swords sound very suspicious.'

'He never said *how* the cargo had been broached,' said Winchester. 'I still say I'm right about evaporation.'

'The Attorney-General didn't *say* a great many things,' said Pisani reflectively. 'In fact, he was far more damaging in what he left unsaid.'

'What can we do?' demanded Winchester.

'About what?' asked Cornwell and the owner realised that both the lawyers and the consul were regarding him curiously.

'In the name of God, surely you don't believe I'm in any way involved in the disappearance of the captain and crew of one of my own vessels!'

'Sorry,' apologised Cornwell. 'It was the phrasing of the question.'

'I meant,' said Winchester, the clarity of his pronunciation and explanation indicating his annoyance at the other's doubts, 'what can be done to prevent this from turning into a kangaroo court?'

Cornwell looked enquiringly at Sprague, who moved his shoulders in a gesture of helplessness.

'Very little,' admitted the Consul. 'Frederick Solly Flood is a man of some established standing in this colony and is the duly appointed Attorney-General. By many he's regarded as a worthy advocate. Personally I regard him as a man with far too vivid an

43

imagination, but Sir James Cochrane seems intent on giving him his head. And he's the duly appointed judge.'

'So I have to sit there, day after day, while the damned man fabricates evidence to suit his convictions.'

'Come now,' protested Cornwell. 'It can't get quite as desperate as that.'

'Can't it!' said the owner. 'I don't recall your attempts to set things right being favourably received today.'

'No,' conceded the lawyer. 'The court feeling is certainly against us.'

'What about this bloodstained sword?' said Winchester.

'I knew of the existence of the sword, from the inventory prepared by the court marshal,' said Cornwell. 'The suggestions of bloodstains came as a complete surprise to me.'

'And not just on the sword. On the decking as well,' Sprague reminded them. He'd been so sure of finding some logical reason for his friends' disappearance; even hoped a ship would arrive somewhere with them aboard and then the whole episode could have been explained. Now he was unsure.

'Do you know Captain Morehouse?' Cornwell asked his client.

'One encounter,' said the ship-owner. 'His reputation is that of being an excellent captain. Why?'

'So you've no reason to doubt his affidavit of how he came upon the vessel and took her into charge?'

The room was completely quiet as Sprague and Winchester considered the implications of the lawyer's question.

'Preposterous!' said Winchester, at last. 'You surely can't propose that a respected captain and crew would slaughter fellow countrymen ... and a baby as well ... in the doubtful expectation of getting $25,000 salvage?'

'They wouldn't have known the value of the cargo,' argued Cornwell. 'They could have imagined it would be something far more valuable and that an award might be higher.'

Captain Winchester smiled for the first time, shaking his head in anticipation of being able to destroy a conjecture.

'But they *would* have known,' he said. 'At the last meeting I had with Captain Briggs before he sailed, he told me he was dining that evening with Captain Morehouse. The men were friends.'

4

Studying his friend, Captain Morehouse pushed his chair back from the tiny cabin table, to enable the steward to clear the meal more easily. Benjamin Briggs was a square-bodied, compact man of whom the initial impression was one of prudent neatness. Although worn comparatively long, as if to compensate for his high forehead, the man's hair was freshly barbered and the moustache and goatee were trimmed shorter than the usual fashion. The suiting was conservatively cut from durable cloth, chosen more for its length of wear than its comfort, and his nails, short-clipped, were still chipped and his hands hardened with the evidence that he worked his ship as readily as any crew he commanded.

He was a man without mannerisms or need for unnecessary conversation or movement. Captain Morehouse knew there were some who would have regarded Briggs's company as dull, but that was not the reaction the man drew from him.

What then? Morehouse concentrated, seeking a word for his feelings and becoming unhappy with the only one which came to mind. Reassurance seemed illogical. Yet that was how he thought of the other man. Benjamin Briggs was a man in whose presence one felt reassurance, whether on the pitching deck of a ship or in the quiet surroundings of a social evening.

Briggs had minutes before raised his head from the prayer of thanks at the end of the meal. There had been similar gratitude before it began and Morehouse thought that in many people, particularly seamen, the piety would have appeared peculiar or an affectation, maybe even something at which to smirk. But with Briggs it had appeared completely natural. He continued the reflection. Many other people, even of sincere conviction, would have passed up the custom at another's table, to avoid embarrassment or perhaps ridicule. But that would never have occurred to Briggs. He was as uncompromising in his attitude to religion as he was in everything else. Morehouse found him an easy man to admire and like.

He lit his pipe, not bothering to offer the pouch to Briggs, who did not take a pipe.

Morehouse got it properly kindled, then said, 'So tomorrow you're off, the owner-captain.'

'Part-owner captain,' qualified Briggs.

'It was a big step, using your capital and borrowing more.'

'I discussed it thoroughly with Sarah. She encouraged it.'

'You like Captain Winchester?'

Briggs considered the question. 'No reason to think otherwise,' he said. 'One of the fairest men along the waterfront, from his conduct so far.'

'That's my feeling, too,' said the second man. 'I'll admit an envy for what you've managed.'

'I was only talking of it to Sarah today,' said Briggs distantly. 'It might so easily not have come about.'

'How so?'

'There was a time when I thought of the church ... family influence, I suppose. And childhood impressions. I lived in a pastor's house for four years.'

'What stopped you?'

'The common sense of my father.'

'He talked you out of it?'

Briggs smiled. 'He was far too wise for that. He just let the infatuation run its course. I served as altar boy and general helper in my grandfather's church and then realised like everyone else what my feelings really were. I don't think I would have had the courage to become a priest.'

Morehouse put his head to one side, considering the statement. Most would have thought that being a sea captain required more bravery than being a country pastor. Briggs was a wise man as well as a pious one.

'I never had any doubts,' said Morehouse. 'In Nova Scotia there seemed no other career but that of the sea and I first shipped out

46

when I was sixteen. Discovered I had a natural aptitude and got my master's certificate when I was twenty-one.'

Briggs added coffee to his cup from a pot the steward had left upon the table.

'Like to buy into ownership one day?' he asked.

'It's my dearest ambition,' confessed Morehouse. 'But establishing the initial capital is the difficulty. There's enough ways of raising money along this and any other coast if you are prepared to load at dusk and dawn, but to do it honestly requires more luck.'

'I had the benefit of a good pursekeeper behind me,' said Briggs.

'Which gives you the advantage over me,' said Morehouse.

Briggs stared down into his coffee cup, apparently in thought, then looked up again. 'Would you like to make the acquaintance of Captain Winchester?' he said. 'I could easily provide a letter of introduction.'

'It's a considerate thought,' said Morehouse. 'But to little purpose, unless I'm backed by money.'

'You've nothing to lose,' argued Briggs. 'Captain Winchester is wiser than either of us in the ways of commerce. Perhaps he'll have a suggestion as to how you could establish capital. I know from my meetings with him that he's keen to meet trustworthy men.'

'I appreciate the compliment,' said Morehouse.

'Will you take the letter then?' demanded Briggs.

Morehouse considered it for several moments.

'Why not?' he said. 'It'll be a contact made, if nothing else.'

Unhappy with the taste of his pipe after their meal of boiled beef, Morehouse tapped the dottle against the ashtray edge and returned it to his pocket.

'Finished loading?' he asked.

'Everything inboard,' said Briggs. 'There's only the final stowage check before sailing.'

'How's your crew?'

'Excellent,' said Briggs. 'I've known Richardson from previous voyages. Andrew Gilling, the second mate, is New York born although of Danish parentage and a good man, already with his first mate's ticket. And one of the Germans has a mate's ticket, too.'

'What's his name?'

'Arien Martens.'

Morehouse nodded. 'He's sailed under me. A first-rate man.'

'Then if the weather improves,' said Briggs, 'it should be an uneventful voyage.'

Morehouse glanced towards the porthole against which the rain was slapping in a constant patter.

'Showing little sign of that,' he said. 'Encountered a schooner captain yesterday who said he'd never known the Atlantic like it. Had to cut their deck cargo adrift and cast it overboard for risk of shifting within days of leaving Plymouth. Now he's involved in an insurance dispute.'

'I'm grateful to have got everything inboard and below decks,' said Briggs. 'What's your shipment?'

'Petroleum, bound for Gibraltar for further orders,' said Morehouse. 'Yours?'

'Commercial alcohol,' said Briggs. 'Genoa and then back with fruit.'

'Any difficulties?'

'Not with the cargo,' said Briggs.

'What then?'

'Holed the main lifeboat a couple of days ago. No way of getting it repaired before we sail. And I can't get a replacement in time.'

Morehouse looked up at his friend curiously.

'You're not sailing without a boat!' he exclaimed.

'Of course not. Captain Winchester had already provided a second, when he learned I was taking Sarah and the baby. And there are the rafts, of course.'

'Worried?'

'No cause to be. I'm charting as southerly a route as possible. It might add a little to our time, but I might miss some of the worst weather.'

'You sail tomorrow?'

'Hopefully,' agreed Briggs.

'I'm heading northerly, which should give me some time over you,' said Morehouse. 'Even though I'm sailing after you we might make Gibraltar around about the same time.'

'I'm estimating the last week of November, maybe the first week of December,' said Briggs.

'Then we should meet,' said Morehouse.

Briggs pulled the pocket watch from his waistcoat. He had promised his wife he would not be late.

'I know Sarah would delight in repaying your hospitality,' he said.

'It was a pity she couldn't come as well.'

'She was sorry, too. But with the strangeness of being aboard ship, we felt it best she remained with Sophia.'

'Arthur sad he couldn't accompany you?'

'Very,' said Briggs. 'And so are we. We don't like the family split. But his education is obviously more important.'

'Does he want to follow the family tradition and take to the sea?'

'At the moment,' smiled Briggs, 'his only ambition is to become an Indian fighter.'

Morehouse joined in the amusement: 'What's your reaction to that?'

Briggs's smile slipped away. ' "Thou shalt not kill",' he quoted. He smiled again, before his friend had time to become discomfited: 'Not even if someone is chasing you with a tomahawk.'

He pushed his chair from the table, rising.

'Sarah will be waiting,' he said. He extended his hand.

'I'll despatch the letter to you before we sail and write to Captain Winchester, telling him to expect a call upon him.'

'You're very kind, Benjamin,' said Morehouse.

In such weather, it was too far to walk from the Erie Basin, where the *Dei Gratia* was moored, to Pier 50 and so Captain Briggs took a carriage. Even so, he got very wet during the short run from the dockside to the *Mary Celeste*.

Sarah was waiting for him, bent over her needle, the lamp casting a yellow glow over her auburn hair. She was very beautiful, decided Briggs, recognising the near-constant thought. Sarah would be embarrassed if she knew how frequently he thought of her; just as he would have been embarrassed to tell her. But she knew, he suspected. Just as he was sure of her feelings about him.

'I don't think the rain will ever stop,' she said, as he stripped off his overcoat and hat. 'Was it a good evening?'

'Boiled beef and excellent greens,' said Briggs. 'Morehouse has got a good cook aboard.'

He looked at Sophia's dress that his wife was mending, then at her sewing machine in the corner.

'Why by hand?'

She nodded towards the tiny cot from which came faint stirrings of the baby girl.

'I thought the noise might disturb her.'

'She'll have to get used to noise, during the voyage,' he said.

'Let's wait until the voyage,' said his wife. She watched him go to his desk and take out his writing case.

'What are you doing?'

'I promised Morehouse I would write him a letter of introduction to Captain Winchester. I'll send a letter to Winchester as well, warning him to expect an approach.'

'Why?'

'Morehouse is keen to buy into a company, like us. I thought Winchester might enjoy meeting him.'

'Does he have any money?'

'No, but Captain Winchester might know a way.'

Sarah bent over her mending and Briggs settled at his desk to write his letters. Almost ten minutes passed before the woman spoke again.

'Do you like Morehouse?' she asked suddenly.

Briggs looked up from his correspondence, frowning.

'Like him?' he echoed. 'That's an odd question.'

'Do you?' she persisted.

'Of course,' said Briggs. 'He's a friend of mine. We've known each other almost since we went to sea. Why do you ask?'

She went back to her mending, considering her reply.

'There have been times,' she said, 'when I felt he was jealous of you.'

He laughed, a disbelieving sound:

'David Morehouse, jealous of me! Shame on you for harbouring such thoughts, Sarah. He's our friend.'

'I've my reservations,' said the woman stubbornly.

'If there's any envy, it's my marriage to you.'

She made a movement of irritation.

'No,' she said. 'Trust me at least to be able to recognise that. It's not our marriage he covets. It's your success.'

Now it was Briggs's turn to show annoyance.

'I consider David Morehouse to be my friend,' he repeated warningly.

'I felt you should know my feelings,' she said, aware she had gone too far.

'And now you must know mine. I never want this discussion to arise between us again.'

She remained with her head lowered over her mending.

'Further,' continued Briggs, 'there's a strong chance of our encountering the *Dei Gratia* in Gibraltar. If we are in port at the same time, I've invited him to dine with us. I want him made welcome at our table.'

'Of course,' she said.

'Properly welcome, Sarah,' he insisted.

She looked up at him.

'I'm sorry I've annoyed you, husband,' she said. 'You know I'll make your friend properly welcome. And never doubt him again.'

'*Our* friend,' Briggs corrected her.

'As you say,' accepted Sarah. 'Our friend.'

Frederick Solly Flood knew himself to be a man of some confidence (although he would have angrily disdained conceit) but prided himself, too, that it was an attitude always tempered with the proper objectivity.

And objectively he accepted that the previous day he had been bested. Not worryingly so. Nor to a degree to affect the final outcome of the enquiry. Indeed, few people present would have recognised it with the honesty he was showing. But by the standards he set himself—and by which he was known and respected within the community of Gibraltar—the Attorney-General did not consider he had sufficiently controlled Captain Winchester as a witness.

Still objective, he realised the fault was none but his own. He had insufficiently anticipated the deviousness of the man, which was a grave mistake. He should have appreciated that a mind capable of evolving a scheme the true extent of which they still had to learn—and he was increasingly convinced that Captain Winchester *was* involved—would not be easily upset no matter how probing the questions.

Continuing his self-analysis, Flood knew that he was a man to learn from his mistakes. And he was determined not to repeat the errors of the previous day.

And they would be easy to avoid, he decided, looking up from his table as Captain Morehouse came to the end of the evidence through which he had been guided by his counsel, Henry Pisani. Captain Winchester was a different cut from this man: Morehouse was a sailor, more used to a quarter-deck than a boardroom.

At the invitation from Cochrane, Flood rose more purposefully this time, without the pantomime of unpreparedness. Morehouse was a man to be influenced by determination rather than lulled by vagueness.

'You knew the destination of the *Mary Celeste*?' he demanded abruptly.

'Yes.'

'From your night-before-sailing dinner with Captain Briggs?'

'Yes.'

'And had even arranged a convivial evening, here in Gibraltar?'

'I have already given evidence as such.'

'Indeed you have, Captain Morehouse. And to that dinner party, the night before the *Mary Celeste* was to sail upon this now infamous voyage, we will return later, but for the moment I want you to assist me on some technical matters.'

Morehouse was regarding him uncertainly, the Attorney-General realised. Almost as if he were frightened.

'I will assist as best I can.'

'An assurance for which I am sure this court is grateful, Captain Morehouse. From that dinner party, as you have attested, you knew the destination of the *Mary Celeste*?'

'Captain Briggs told me Genoa.'

'Quite so. And before that, Gibraltar?'

'Yes.'

'So you could estimate, from your expertise as a master-mariner, his likely course?'

'We discussed it,' said Morehouse. 'In view of the continued gales and storms of which we were getting reports before we left New York and the fact that he had his family aboard, Captain Briggs intended to set a southerly course.'

'Remind the court, if you will, of your setting when you came upon the *Mary Celeste* on December 5.'

'I've already given that.'

'I asked you to remind the court again, Captain Morehouse.'

'Latitude 38.20 N. by longitude 17.15 W.,' said Morehouse.

Despite the man's full, almost theatrical beard, Flood recognised the slight burst of colour to Morehouse's face at the reminder of who was conducting the questioning. And his eyes seemed to be staring more obviously from his face. Flood judged Morehouse to be a man of violent temper.

'You are a master of some experience?'

'I have been qualified for the past thirteen years,' said More-house, the pride obvious.

'A fine record,' said Flood genially. 'Now, from the experience of those thirteen years, advise the enquiry of a likely setting for a vessel taking a southerly course from New York, en route for Gibraltar, some eighteen days after departure.'

Morehouse frowned, looking to Pisani. Flood was aware of the other lawyer's unhelpful shrug.

'Roughly that upon which I came upon the vessel,' said More-house. 'Although when we closed to the *Mary Celeste* she was sailing back upon herself, westwards, not eastwards as she should have been if the Straits of Gibraltar were her heading.'

'Remind the court again, if you will, Captain Morehouse, of the date inscribed upon the slate-log found by one of your men after boarding.'

'Eight in the morning of November 25,' said the captain.

'Ten days before, according to the evidence that you have presented to this court, you came upon the vessel?'

'Yes.'

'How was she set?'

'Her rigging and sheets were in great disarray,' said Morehouse, his face creased with the effort of recollection. 'What I first took upon the sighting through my glass to be a distress signal subsequently turned out to be a flapping sail, torn from its mast. What first struck me as peculiar was that although her jib and fore-topmast staysail were set upon the starboard tack, she was sailing upon the port tack, yawing as she came into the wind and then falling off again. I watched her doing that for two hours.'

'What about the other sails?'

'When we got close enough, I could see that her mainsail, gaff-topsail, middle staysail, topmast staysail, top-gallant sail, royal and flying jib were all furled.'

'So what remained?'

'Her main staysail appeared to have been hurriedly collapsed. The foresail and upper fore-topsail had been blown away. And the lower fore-topsail was hanging by the four corners. It was that which I had first taken to be the distress signal.'

'A squall weather setting, in fact?'

'Yes,' agreed Morehouse doubtfully. 'It could be described as such.'

'What were the weather conditions on December 5 and the days immediately prior to that?'

'Squally.'

'How far had the *Mary Celeste* sailed from the slate-log entry of November 25 until December 5, when you came upon her?'

'It's impossible to know the distance,' said Morehouse, 'but I would estimate some 378 miles.'

For the first time during his cross-examination, Flood bent over his papers, creating a pause for what he was going to say. He actually waited until he could detect shufflings of impatience from those behind him in the chamber before looking up again:

'Help me further, Captain Morehouse, if you will, over something I find quite remarkable. Indeed, utterly and completely inexplicable ... '

Flood allowed another break, to unsettle the man he was questioning.

'Utilising all the experience and expertise that you have amassed during the thirteen years you have been a master-mariner, tell me how the *Mary Celeste*, more or less properly set for the prevailing conditions, came to be more or less precisely on course when, if the evidence you have presented to this enquiry is correct, the last log entry of any kind had been some ten days earlier, on November 25?' Flood smiled up, ingenuously, content with the trap into which he had manoeuvred the witness. 'How had the *Mary Celeste* sailed, unmanned, for 378 miles and remained on course, Captain Morehouse?' he completed, his voice hardening.

'I don't know,' said Morehouse abruptly.

'You don't know!' demanded Flood, pushing the incredulity into his voice.

'How can I?' protested the man.

'A point we might later attempt to elucidate,' said the Attorney-General, and before Morehouse could respond, added: 'Have you ever before heard of an unmanned vessel, with sails set for the prevailing weather, cover nearly four hundred miles and remain on course?'

'No.'

Flood bent over his papers, for his own benefit on this occasion.

Whatever the faults of the previous day's examination, he had recovered now, he decided. With the major – and in his view the most devastating – part of his cross-examination still to come he had already proved Morehouse's evidence illogical to the point of falsity. The satisfaction warmed through him.

'I seek further assistance, Captain Morehouse,' he started again, smiling up. 'The prevailing currents in this part of the Atlantic, to my amateur eye, appear to be southwards.'

'That is so,' agreed Morehouse uncomfortably.

'Cast your mind back to your recent crossing, if you will,' Flood invited him. 'What was the prevailing wind?'

'Predominantly from the north,' conceded Morehouse, frowning in his awareness of the point of Flood's questioning.

'So the mystery deepens,' gloated Flood. 'Not only does the unmanned *Mary Celeste* remain on course for ten days, but she does so against the prevailing currents and winds.'

'I made allowances for that in calculating the distance she might have covered,' said Morehouse. 'And it is not necessarily surprising that such a thing could have happened.'

'Ah,' exclaimed the Attorney-General, completely sure of his control, 'you have an answer to this conundrum!'

'Not an answer,' conceded Morehouse. 'A possible explanation.'

'Then let's have it, Captain Morehouse. Let's have it.'

'Dismasted, a vessel might expect to be carried in the direction of the tide and the wind,' said Morehouse. 'But, as I have already given evidence, some of the *Mary Celeste*'s sails were still set.'

'So?' prompted Flood.

'When I came upon her,' said Morehouse, 'she was yawing as she came into the wind and then falling off again. It is a recognised fact that whether there is anyone at the helm or not, a sailing ship, under some sail, will hold up into the wind and not drift with the wind or current. The setting of the fore-topmast staysail and jib would have had the effect of preventing her coming into the wind, keeping her more steadily on course.'

'Are you seriously inviting this enquiry to accept that, almost by some divine intervention, the setting of the sails was such that they actually kept the *Mary Celeste against* prevailing wind and sea conditions!' said Flood, turning as he asked the question from the judge to the court, as if inviting them to share his amazement.

'It has been known,' insisted Morehouse doggedly.

'You can give the court an example?'

'Sir?'

'You can quote to Sir James and the rest of this enquiry an actual stated case of an abandoned, rigged vessel completing the manoeuvre you suggest in this part of the Atlantic?'

'No,' admitted Morehouse, face burning with discomfort. 'I was speaking in the most general terms about conditions that have been experienced by sailors.'

'This enquiry, Captain Morehouse, is not interested in the most general terms about what might or might not have befallen unnamed ships on unnamed oceans. It is concerned about what befell the *Mary Celeste* when she was but six miles from the island of Santa Maria on the morning of November 25.'

'I am aware of that, sir,' said Morehouse, attempting to regain his dignity.

'Then let us apply ourselves a little more diligently to uncovering the truth of the matter,' said the Attorney-General. He had discredited Morehouse, he decided confidently. He could more or less dictate the responses now, just as the British soldiers trained the apes to perform for the tourists high above on the mist-shrouded Peak.

'Let us cast ourselves back to the meal you enjoyed with Captain Briggs the night before his sailing,' said Flood. 'It was a convivial evening between two old friends?'

'That's how I think of it,' said Morehouse.

'There was no point for the meeting, apart from that of conviviality?'

'No,' said Morehouse. 'We had been friends for many years. Whenever we were in port together, we always attempted a meeting. At that dinner in New York, we arranged a meal here.'

'So you have already informed us. Be more forthcoming, if you would. What else was discussed that night?'

Morehouse did not immediately respond, head cast down in the effort of recall.

'As I remember,' he said, 'a great deal of the talk was of Captain Briggs becoming part-owner of the *Mary Celeste*.'

'He was rightfully proud?'

'He was. I owned that I envied him his success.'

'Envied him!' snatched Flood. Here it was, he thought. The first slip.

Imagining a mistake, Morehouse looked to his counsel, who stared back curiously.

'He asked me if I sought to be in the same position as he was. And I admitted I did.'

'Tell me, Captain Morehouse,' said the Attorney-General, spacing his words so that they would be recognised as an important part of the evidence, while trying at the same time to remove any indication of the satisfaction he felt, 'what prevents you from doing what Captain Briggs did and becoming a part-owner?'

Part-owner, remembered Morehouse. Benjamin's constant qualification, determined as the man had always been against self-aggrandisement. Why was it, wondered Morehouse, that an innocent gathering between friends was capable of the sinister interpretations upon which this tiny, hurried little man seemed intent?

'Capital,' he said, aware before he spoke of how his questioner would turn the answer. 'One has to buy one's way into ownership.'

'And you had no money?'

'No.'

'What was Captain Briggs's response to that?'

'He provided me with a letter of introduction to Captain Winchester.'

The Attorney-General slowly twisted, encompassing first the witness and then the New York owner who had given evidence the previous day and who sat today leaning forward in his seat, note pad upon his knee. The Attorney-General thought Captain Winchester looked worried. With every reason, he decided: he had uncovered the link between the two men.

'So he brought you and Captain Winchester together?'

'Yes.'

'To what purpose?'

Morehouse shrugged. 'Little more than establishing contact between us. Captain Briggs said Captain Winchester was always ready to meet reliable masters and that he might know of a way that I could raise capital sufficient for my needs.'

' ... "capital sufficient for my needs",' quoted Flood. He stopped, letting the inference settle. Then he said, 'Tell me, Captain Morehouse, what do you consider would be capital sufficient for your needs?'

'That's a hypothetical question' said the captain, in vain protest.

'Just as a rigged fore-topmast staysail and jib keeping an unmanned vessel against tide and wind is a hypothetical solution to this mystery,' said the Attorney-General. 'What do you consider would be capital sufficient for your needs?'

'No figure was ever discussed at my meeting with Captain Winchester,' said Morehouse. He was shifting from foot to foot, like a child seeking a teacher's permission to leave the classroom.

'What do you consider would be capital sufficient for your needs?' persisted Flood.

'Perhaps $5,000. Perhaps more ... '

'Perhaps $5,000. Perhaps more,' echoed Flood. 'Are you an ambitious man?'

As on the previous day, the man's counsel finally intervened, rising hurriedly from his seat.

'Sir!' protested Pisani to Cochrane. 'The direction in which my friend is seeking to lead this examination must be clear to everyone at this enquiry, a direction for which no evidence whatsoever has so far been produced for your consideration. Surely it is wrong during the hearing of a civil matter, which this is, to permit behaviour more in keeping with a Star Chamber.'

Just as Pisani's objection had been so similar to that of his fellow lawyers, so the judge's response was comparable. His head came up from his bench, face suffused and red.

'Star Chamber!' he said.

Pisani appeared less in awe of the man than the lawyer representing the owner.

'A term invoked after some consideration,' he said.

'You, sir, are impudent,' said Cochrane.

'And I fear, sir, that you endanger the reputation of your court if you permit the conduct of this case to proceed in its present manner,' said Pisani.

'I have already made it clear how I intend this enquiry to proceed,' said Cochrane. 'I will allow no interference in the search for the truth.'

'None of us here would object to the pursuit of the truth,' said the lawyer. 'My objection is in the pursuit of preconceptions and innuendo.'

'I have listened with the utmost consideration to everything said since the beginning of this enquiry,' said the judge, with obviously enforced evenness. 'And so far I have detected nothing which has caused me even to consider questioning the behaviour of the Attorney-General ... ' He hesitated. 'And I would remind you, Mr Pisani, that my jurisdiction here is absolute and that I am answerable to no court of appeal but to their Lords of the Admiralty.'

'A fact which has not escaped my attention. Nor my concern,' said the lawyer. He looked towards the registrar.

'I trust my observations have been noted and entered into the court record,' he said.

Baumgartner twisted nervously towards Cochrane, who said curtly, 'As I have already mentioned, sir, everything at this hearing is being noted ... ' He turned his head, to Flood: 'Pray continue, Mr Attorney-General.'

'At what age did you attain the rank of captain?' Flood asked Morehouse, rising from the bench at which he had sat during the exchange between the judge and the man's lawyer.

'Twenty-one,' said Morehouse.

'A young man?'

'Yes.'

'A very young man?'

'Comparatively so.'

'Would you describe yourself as an ambitious man?' he asked again.

'It is not a question I have considered, sir.'

'Then put your mind to it now. Are you an ambitious man?'

'I do not consider myself to be any more ambitious than most.'

'Tell the enquiry, Captain Morehouse, what is your age now?' said Flood. With every prevarication, the man worsened his credibility.

'Thirty-four.'

'A captain at twenty-one, still just a captain thirteen years later.'

'An achievement with which I am content enough,' said Morehouse.

'Really, sir!' said Flood. 'Not thirty minutes ago, the word you used was envy.'

Morehouse lifted his arm, a motion of confusion.

'A loose use of words. I did not intend to convey that I coveted anything that Benjamin Briggs had achieved. Rather, that I admired the man for having attained so much.'

'An attainment you did not seek to emulate?'

Morehouse sighed, resigned. 'Of course I would welcome advancement,' he said. 'But not in the manner that you are suggesting.'

'What manner am I suggesting?'

'You seek to turn innocent talk into incriminating discussion ... to find suspicion in anything for which there is not a ready solution ... '

'I seek only the truth,' insisted the Attorney-General. 'Unpalatable though it may be ... '

'I have assisted you in every way I can,' protested Morehouse desperately.

'A little more, I beg you,' said Flood, in mock humility. 'Before the recent discussion between My Lord and Mr Pisani, we were talking of capital. We had agreed, I believe, that $5,000 would have been sufficient for you to purchase yourself at least part-ownership of a vessel in Captain Winchester's company?'

'No!' said the witness, gazing for help first to Cochrane and then to his lawyer. 'I was repeating the vaguest of conversations ... giving little more than my own estimate of what I might need to come to any agreement. There was no talk between Captain Winchester and myself about any such agreement.'

'Were this salvage claim to succeed, would you anticipate that your proportion of any money awarded would be in excess of $5,000?'

'I've not considered an amount,' said Morehouse thoughtlessly.

Flood did not take up the remark immediately, allowing them all to recognise the man's mistake for themselves.

'I, for one, do not believe the truth of that answer,' the Attorney-General said finally. 'Any more than I expect the majority of people present at this enquiry believe it. To give you the advantage of correcting an impression of falsehood, I shall repeat the question. Were this salvage claim to succeed, would you anticipate that your share of any award would be in excess of $5,000?'

'Yes,' said Morehouse, his voice little more than a whisper.

'Sufficient for a partnership?'

Morehouse looked up, staring intently at the Attorney-General with his prominent eyes.

'I regarded Captain Briggs as one of my closest friends,' he said pleadingly. 'I would have done nothing to hurt him.'

'I never said that you had, Captain Morehouse.'

'You suggested it.'

'No, sir, it was not I who suggested it. It is your evidence this enquiry has been considering this day.'

Morehouse said nothing. He was having difficulty in controlling himself, Flood realised.

'Isn't the proper explanation for your finding of the *Mary Celeste* that she remained crewed after November 25, the date of the last official log entry?'

'Who knows ... ?' Morehouse began, generalising, but Flood intervened:

'That's what I'm endeavouring to discover,' he pressed. 'And having remained manned, was on course for a rendezvous?'

'But –' tried Morehouse again.

'A rendezvous with a vessel that would put the crew who had mutinied and foully murdered the captain and his family safely ashore somewhere, later to share in any salvage claim?'

'But *we* salvaged the *Mary Celeste*,' said Morehouse, not fully comprehending.

'Indeed you did,' said Flood.

'No!' shouted the man, understanding at last. 'That's a monstrous suggestion.'

'What is monstrous is what happened to Captain Briggs, his wife and baby daughter,' said the Attorney-General.

Because of the restrictions upon land available, there were few imposing residences in Gibraltar, but Flood's was one of the grandest that conditions would permit. It was a low, two-storey building with a view of the linking peninsula and the mainland beyond, arranged Spanish-style around a tree-shaded courtyard the centrepiece of which was a fountain-filled pool.

From shareholding in ships' chandlery, freight and import business, the conduct of which was scrupulously watched and open to public examination, so that he could never be accused of conflict of interest, Flood was a rich man and he enjoyed his wealth. Since the death of his wife, the house was too large and there were more servants than he needed either to maintain it or to take care of his needs, but he retained both, knowing his public position required it.

Having already taken a glass with Sir James Cochrane, the Attorney-General restricted himself to one tot of sherry while he awaited the man whose evidence would create a sensation. It had been difficult for him to restrain himself from advising in advance the journalists who were treating him so kindly in their publications.

Flood sipped his wine, savouring the flavour, thinking of the enquiry. The invitations to the judge's chambers after each session appeared to be becoming established as a regular routine. And tonight's encounter had been easier than the first. 'Undoubtedly suspicious,' Cochrane had said. Which Flood considered a mild judgment. He'd established a motive for the murder of Captain Briggs and his family; Morehouse to get sufficient funds from a salvage claim to set himself up in ownership and Captain Winchester to share the award while at the same time retaining ship and cargo, thus showing an extra profit and losing nothing. And it hadn't stopped there. As well as a motive, he'd obtained from their own mouths the admission that the two men had known each other and had met after Captain Briggs had sailed from New York. It was fitting together very nicely.

He put his glass down upon a verandah table, his satisfaction marred by the recollection of another remark from Cochrane. Suspicious, the judge had agreed. But had then warned of the continued absence of any positive evidence. Immediately, Flood brightened. That wouldn't be long arriving.

As if prompted by his thoughts, there was movement behind and a maid ushered Dr Patron on to the verandah.

Flood rose to meet the analyst, hand extended.

'Some refreshment here, or shall we get to work straight away in the study?' the Attorney-General invited him.

'Much as I should like to admire this superb view,' said the chemist, 'I do have appointments to fulfil. So I'm afraid it must be work.'

Glad of the man's refusal to waste time, Flood led the way from the verandah to a room at the back of the house. Dr Patron followed, briefcase held protectively in front of him, as if it contained something very valuable.

'You've prepared the report?' demanded Flood eagerly, as soon as the other man was seated.

Patron reached into the briefcase and took out two bound, closely written folios, pushing one across the desk.

'Encapsulate it for me,' insisted the Attorney-General.

The doctor fitted half-lens glasses into place and then took from the briefcase his original copy of the report, for reference.

'At your request,' he began formally, 'I boarded the *Mary Celeste* in the forenoon of the 30th. The express purpose was to ascertain whether any marks or stains could be discovered on or in her hulk –'

'And ... ?' prompted Flood impatiently.

The analyst frowned, irritated at the attempt to hurry him.

'I made a careful study and minute inspection of the vessel,' he said. 'On the deck in the forepart of the vessel I found some brown spots about a millimetre thick and half an inch in diameter. These I separated from the deck with a chisel. In all I found spotting sufficient to make up four exhibit envelopes. There was a further, similar spot on the top-gallant rail. I made an exhibit from that, as I did from that piece of timber provided by you ... '

Flood smiled. It had been he who had first seen the marked timber and insisted upon Thomas Vecchio, the marshal, cutting it out during their first visit to the *Mary Celeste*.

'Apart from these spots, I could find nothing within the vessel to suggest any bloodstaining,' continued Dr Patron. 'Later during my examination I received from Mr Vecchio the sword and scabbard, which he informed me had been found beneath the bunk in the captain's cabin.'

Flood sighed, exasperated by the man's pedantic presentation, but he suppressed the urge to hurry him.

'Three spots I had obtained from the deck were large enough to hang upon threads before suspending them in tubes containing a quantity of distilled water. Two others were so small that I had to put them into filtering bags before commencing the maceration –'

'How long did it take?' demanded Flood, anticipating the result.

Again there was a frown from the chemist at the other man's urgency.

'The initial maceration was continued for two and a quarter hours,' he said. 'At the end of that time, the distilled water was as clear and bright as it had been at the commencment of the experiment.'

The Attorney-General tilted his head to one side in one of his bird-like positions, as if it were difficult to understand what the other man was saying.

'Notwithstanding that, I left things as they were until the following day, but even at the end of twenty-four hours there was still no discoloration of the water. I then heated the exhibits by spirit lamp, but still there was no cloudy aspect forthcoming –'

'Are you telling me ... ?'

'I then concluded that particular experiment, believing it to be negative,' said the doctor, refusing the interruption. 'I then put beneath the microscope those particles I had attempted to macerate in filtering bags. I identified carbonate of iron and a vegetable substance –'

'I'm a layman, doctor. What is that?'

'Rust,' said Patron simply. 'And wood fibres.'

'The sword,' said Flood urgently. 'What about the sword?'

Patron nodded. 'About the middle and rear part of the blade were stains of a more suspicious character,' he resumed. 'Although small and superficial, their aspect was reddish and in some parts brilliant. My first impression was that they were unquestionably bloodstains.'

Missing the qualification, Flood began nodding, sharp, abrupt movements.

'I subjected them to the same maceration as I had attempted with the earlier experiments, once again submitting them to heat when no discoloration of the liquid took place. There was still no clouding under conditions of heat. Under a microscope, I identified an imperfectly crystallised substance resembling citrate of iron. Three other stains were tested with hydrochloric acid and after a perceptible effervescence a yellow stain was produced of chloride of iron —'

The Attorney-General jerked up from the desk no longer able to contain his patience.

'The examination was to prove bloodstaining, doctor,' he said. 'What about the blood?'

Dr Patron stared up, aware for the first time that the other man had not properly assimilated what he was saying.

'There was no blood,' he said.

The Attorney-General had started to walk around from the desk, towards a window. Now he stopped, frowning back at the analyst:

'No blood?'

'Not present in any of the experiments I conducted from the material I took from the vessel. And had any of that spotting from the deck or the stains to the sword been blood, it would have registered during the maceration.'

'But it *must* be blood,' insisted Flood, refusing the other man's word.

'Rust,' Dr Patron corrected him.

'What other tests did you carry out?' persisted Flood.

'I did not consider that any more were necessary. Blood would have registered had it been present during my examination.'

'What about solvents?'

'I could have attempted a reaction from solvents,' conceded the analyst. 'But as I have said, I did not consider it necessary.'

'But *I* consider it necessary,' said Flood, making an effort to control his temper. 'I would like you to return to your laboratory and subject those exhibits to further analysis.'

'That isn't possible,' said Patron uncomfortably.

'I don't understand,' said Flood.

'I have disposed of the samples,' said Patron. Aware of the colour reaching the Attorney-General's face, he hurried on: 'It was a failed experiment, producing nothing. I did not imagine you would want them preserved ... there was no point —'

'You destroyed them!'

Flood shouted in his outrage.

'They had no usefulness,' Patron tried, awkwardly.

'They were court exhibits, Dr Patron. Made so by their being

67

handed to you by a duly sworn official of the court. You've destroyed court evidence. Worse, you'd destroyed it before carrying out properly the task with which you were entrusted.'

'I believe I fulfilled every function with which I was charged,' said Patron defiantly. 'There was *no* blood.'

Many years before, soon after he had arrived in the colony, Flood had climbed with some other young men to the very tip of the Peak and then they had all stood aloft to stare into Spain to their left and out across the Mediterranean to their right. For the first time he had learned that he suffered from vertigo: ever since, by closing his eyes, Flood had been able to recall that stomach-emptying sensation of helplessness at the conviction that he was going to topple thousands of feet into the water below. It had taken his companions nearly five hours, at times blindfolding him, to bring him safely down. Flood closed his eyes now, without calling the incident to mind, and the impression of dropping into space was very real. He suddenly realised that there were no further samples for another analysis. Anxious to provide Dr Patron with every available particle, he had ensured that everything suspicious had been scraped from the deck during their visits. And now the confounded man had thrown it all away.

'Are you aware, Dr Patron, that because of your crass incompetence you have endangered the proving of an undoubted crime?' he said, his voice jagged in his rage.

'I do not accept incompetence,' said Patron, in matching anger. 'I carried out the accepted tests upon the material with which I was supplied and reached a negative finding.'

'Didn't it occur to you that I might seek a second opinion?'

'There would have been little point. The conclusion would have been that which I reached.'

'You compound your incompetence by arrogance!' said Flood, voice loud again. 'How can you say what someone else might have found using methods different from those which you chose to employ?'

'I am confident of my report,' insisted Patron, pointing to the paper which lay as he had put it upon the Attorney-General's desk.

The complete awareness of how the analyst had damaged the case he was attempting to pursue swept through the Attorney-

General. So, too, did the feeling of impotence at his inability to correct it.

'I could have you arraigned before the enquiry to answer for this,' he said vehemently. But he wouldn't take such a course, he accepted. even as he made the threat. Because it would provide an escape route for all those whose guilt he now had to prove by other methods.

'I will not be threatened,' said the other man. 'I carried out the task entrusted to me to the best of my ability. It is not my fault it failed to register positively.'

'It is *precisely* your fault, Dr Patron,' said Flood.

'This is the very first occasion upon which my professional ability has been challenged,' said Patron.

And it would be the last, determined Flood. He would never again employ Patron upon any experiment. And he'd make damned sure that few others did, either.

Anxious now to end the encounter, Patron took a diary from his briefcase, opening it officiously.

'I'd appreciate some indication of when you'd like me to appear,' he said stiffly.

Flood frowned at him. 'What?'

'A date for me to give evidence at the enquiry.'

Flood experienced another surge of rage, this time at the thought of how eagerly the other lawyers would seize and twist the analyst's evidence.

'I am undecided if that will be necessary, in view of the negative nature of the results,' said Flood. Seeing the look of surprise upon the man's face, he added heavily: 'I would imagine that questions about the missing exhibits might become a little invidious.'

'I devoted a great deal of time and attention to the tests, believing them to be important,' said Patron.

'A pity that even more time was not invested,' said Flood. He moved from his desk, as anxious as the doctor to end the interview. The man was an irritating fool.

The pretence of civility was difficult, but Flood personally accompanied the analyst to the door. A fresh thought halted him just inside: the advantage to the other advocates, if they became aware of the inconclusive evidence. He seized Patron's arm:

'You appreciate, of course, that even though it has not been officially produced, your report remains a court document, commissioned as it was by me?'

'I don't understand,' said the man doubtfully.

'It's contents are *sub judice*, to be discussed with no one,' said the Attorney-General.

'Oh.'

'In fact, it could be construed as a punishable offence to reveal your findings unless so permitted by the judge.'

'I see,' said the doctor.

'To no one,' emphasised the Attorney-General.

'No one,' agreed Dr Patron.

Flood stood at the door, watching the man enter his carriage, then turned back into the house. Unthinkingly, he walked back to the verandah and sat where he had done before the man's arrival, gazing out over the bay.

Again he was swept by the nauseous sensation of falling into emptiness. He clenched his hands together, fighting against the feeling. On the Peak all those years ago there had been friends aware of his difficulty. This time he had no one to guide him back to safety.

6

Benjamin Briggs was not an unemotional man: in the privacy of their bedroom or night cabin, Sarah found him a considerate but still passionate lover. In his public conduct, however, he was a self-contained, very controlled man. It was not an attitude of shyness. Nor did it come from a lack of outspokenness. The very opposite, in fact. He simply regarded the charades in which people frequently indulged to convey their moods to be unnecessary posturing; a sign of immaturity, even. If Briggs had something to say, he said it. But never with rudeness or malice or without good cause, so that people were rarely offended. And if they were, then Briggs, who was not unfeeling either, considered it unfortunate but unavoidable. He had to be accepted as he was, someone without artifice or affectation.

He stood at the rail of the *Mary Celeste*, staring back at the vague skyline of New York from which they had so recently departed. There were many captains who would have indulged in some after-deck ranting at being beaten back by a head wind within an hour of leaving Pier 50 the previous day and being forced to anchor off Staten Island.

But it would have achieved nothing, except perhaps polite smiles from the crew. He had experienced a moment of passing irritation and then he had dismissed it, just as he had dismissed the initial, fleeting thought of not turning back, but sailing on against the weather. Having Sarah and the baby aboard had not influenced his decision to heave to. It would have been bad seamanship to have gone out into the dirty weather obviously confronting him when there was protective anchorage so close to hand. And Briggs was not a poor seaman.

He was aware that the crew whom he still had to come to know would recognise it as the decision of good captaincy. Briggs was no more interested in impressing them than he was in earning their sycophantic smiles, but he had never forgotten a long-ago lesson from his father on the importance of a captain's achieving the confidence of his men. A confident crew was a good crew. Even more important, an obedient one.

Briggs did not regard it, therefore, as a completely pointless delay, but as time put to some purpose, psychological rather than practical though it might be.

He heard movement behind him and turned as Richardson emerged from the main hatch, followed by the German brothers Volkert and Boz Lorensen.

'Wherever we thought it necessary, we've double-lashed the barrels against movement,' said the first mate.

Briggs gazed beyond the man, out to sea. Although little after midday, the weather was so black that it was impossible to detect the horizon.

'It'll doubtless be a precaution we'll need,' agreed Briggs. The man's initiative pleased him; his order had merely been to check the cargo.

'If it remains like this,' said the first mate, looking in the same direction as the captain, 'there'll be few days when we're not awash.'

'Best double batten the hatches,' said the captain.

'There's already a smell down there,' said Richardson, nodding towards the still-open hold.

'There'll be opportunity to ventilate,' said Briggs confidently. 'I checked the pumps this morning and they're as sound as anyone could want, so I don't anticipate problems no matter how much sea we ship.'

'And according to the log of Captain Spates, there's very little leakage.'

Wind suddenly gusted over the deck and Briggs shivered in the winter cold.

'Let's move to my cabin,' he said.

Before following the captain towards the accommodation door, Richardson told Boz Lorensen to batten the hatchway through which they had just emerged and replace the boat upon its fenders.

Briggs was already at his desk when Richardson entered. The

man made no move to sit until invited to do so by the other man.

'Any annoyance about drink?' Briggs asked, as soon as the man was seated. The day before they had left the pier, Briggs had mustered the crew and told them he would not allow alcohol during the voyage.

'No disgruntlement at all,' said Richardson immediately. 'I was a little surprised.'

'So am I,' admitted the captain.

'It's too early to say, of course, but I don't think we're going to get any trouble with them. They all seem good seamen.'

'Let's hope you're not proved wrong.'

'Aye.'

'From our other voyages together, Mr Richardson, you'll know I'm a man who likes a ship tidy run.'

'I know.'

'I accept it'll sometimes be unavoidable, but I want no cursing, certainly not in the presence of Mrs Briggs.'

'I've already made that clear.'

'And I want it impressed upon them that I meant what I said during muster – I'll not allow gambling. On a vessel this size, it can only lead to dispute.'

'The men understand your order,' Richardson assured Briggs.

'There'll be prayers on Sundays, to which all will be welcome in my day cabin.'

'I'll let it be known,' said Richardson. 'The Germans are Catholic, but they may care to attend.'

'It'll be more to worship God than denominational.'

Richardson nodded. He sat respectfully with his cap upon his knee.

'I'll make Sundays the day for crew quarter inspection, too,' decided Briggs. 'I know it'll be difficult, particularly if the weather stays dirty, but I shall expect the men to take sea showers, of course.'

'They give the appearance of cleanliness.'

'First impressions can sometimes be misleading.'

'True enough,' accepted Richardson.

Briggs sat wondering if the first mate regarded as unduly restrictive the regulations he had imposed for the voyage. He hoped not. In his father, Briggs recognised, he had had a diligent tutor. Not that he had followed the old man's disciplinarianism to the degree that he had practised. Briggs had never heard his father give an order directly to a member of the crew, but always through the mates. And that had applied to any of his sons, when they had sailed under him. Afloat, his family might have been strangers to him.

At sea, no sailor had ever thought of passing him on the weather side when he had been walking the quarter-deck. Going to or from the wheel they always had to go on the lee side and, if there were work to be done on the weather side, no sailor had ever passed the man without touching his cap and always to leeward, never intruding themselves between the old man and the sea.

'The proper etiquette of the sea,' the man had called it. While Briggs felt it important to run an orderly ship, he considered it impractical to be quite so autocratic upon a vessel such as the *Mary Celeste*.

He rose, going to a small chart table beneath the cabin window.

'I'm making a southerly course for Gibraltar,' he said. 'We might find better weather there.'

Realising the invitation, Richardson rose, following him to look down on the charts, upon which Briggs had already pencilled a route.

'What if the weather improves?'

'I might change northerly, but I'll let it set first. I'm not going to alter course at every change of wind.'

'What about a return cargo?' asked Richardson, as they went back to their seats.

'Fruit in Messina,' said Briggs. 'We'll sail as soon as we discharge at Genoa.'

Briggs recalled Richardson's recent marriage to the niece of Captain Winchester and recognised a point to the question.

'When have you set your mind for returning?' he said.

'February or thereabouts,' said the first mate.

'Could even be before, if things run smoothly. Hoping for your own command?'

Richardson nodded. 'Something small, to begin with,' he said. 'Ply around the coast here, perhaps.'

74

'Wife intend sailing with you?'

'As much as possible.'

'Wise decision,' said Briggs. 'It's a lonely life for a woman, being a sailor's wife. Mrs Briggs has sailed with me often.'

'Not easy with children, though.'

'True enough,' accepted Briggs. 'It'll be more difficult when Sophia starts her schooling.'

As if reminded, Richardson looked towards the cabin door.

'Line should be up by now,' he said.

Briggs rose, leading the way from the cabin. As they emerged on deck, Briggs saw Arien Martens, the German whom he knew to hold a mate's certificate, helping the baby into a halter. As he got closer, he saw it had been carefully made from thin rope plaited and then fashioned into a tiny bodice that fitted over Sophia's shoulders, looped criss-cross over her back and then connected with a tiny belt. From the belt another plaited line had been spliced around a metal ring, the other end connected to another metal ring that could run freely along a length of rope that had been strung between the two masts.

Sarah, who was crouched alongside the child, looked up at her husband's approach.

'Look what Mr Martens has made,' said the woman, her delight obvious.

A great deal of care had gone into the construction of the safety line and harness, Briggs realised. He nodded to the sailor.

'It's first-class,' he said. 'Thank you.'

The man jerked his head, almost the beginning of a bowing motion and then clipped the harness into place on the line. Pandering to the attention, Sophia ran the full length between the two masts and then turned, coming back. Briggs frowned, then saw that the connecting line against the bodice ran free along the belt, so that the child could move in both directions instead of having to call for assistance every time she got to the end of the line and wanted to return.

'*Really* first-class,' he said again, to the man. 'Mrs Briggs and I are most grateful.'

Richardson and the sailor moved forwards, towards the hatch over which Boz Lorensen was still hunched, straining to get the boat properly secured. Sophia continued to scuttle about the deck, looking around anxiously to ensure that the attention was still upon her.

'I shall have no fear of Sophia being on deck in that,' said Sarah.

'No,' agreed Briggs.

'I regret not being able to attend church before we sailed,' said Sarah suddenly.

'So do I,' said Briggs, recalling his decision that day on the way to the shipping office. 'But it couldn't be avoided.'

The time he had intended spending in worship had been passed instead in the attempt to find a replacement longboat. He looked to the stern; a holding stay had been looped through the empty davits. Beyond the vessel, he was suddenly aware of the increasing lightness in the sky. He could detect the skyline now.

'Weather's lifting,' he said.

His wife moved close to his side.

'I've got a feeling, Benjamin,' she said.

He looked down to her curiously.

'I've got a feeling that we have got an excellent crew, an excellent boat and that we are going to have an excellent voyage.'

He smiled, enjoying her extravagance.

'This is going to be the beginning of a fine time for us,' insisted the woman. 'It won't be long before it will be "Winchester & Briggs".'

He laughed openly at her.

'I fear there's some way to go before that,' he said. 'We've not one voyage completed yet.'

'I can't see anything that can upset it, can you?'

'No,' he said, 'I can't.'

'Then don't be such a pessimist,' she protested.

'Better if one of us keeps a sound head,' he said, in mock seriousness.

She gazed up at him, her smile became an expression of affection.

'I feel so very secure with you, Benjamin,' she said. 'When I'm with you I never think any harm could befall me.'

He became truly serious.

'I'll see it never does,' he promised.

'Me! Me!'

They turned. Sophia was standing at the end of the line, arms outstretched and face twisted into the beginning of tears at being completely ignored.

Briggs went to her, unclipped the line and took her into his arms.

'You too,' he said, nuzzling the child's hair with his face. 'I'll keep you safe, too.'

'That's great comfort to me,' Sarah said.

He looked at her, not understanding.

'Knowing how well the children would be cared for if anything happened to me,' enlarged the woman.

He looked over the child's shoulder as Richardson moved back along the deck.

'Getting better,' said the first mate, looking out to sea.

'Aye,' said Briggs. 'Prepare to sail.'

Frederick Flood decided it would have taken someone far more astute than any at the enquiry to notice a difference in his demeanour. That there was a difference he accepted readily enough, for just as he had earlier recognised his confidence, he now made a conscious effort to be honest with himself. It was his confidence that had suffered from Dr Patron's visit to his home the previous evening. But just his confidence; certainly not his conviction that crime was at the root of the *Mary Celeste* mystery. The analyst was an incompetent fool who had clearly carried out the wrong experiments. The Attorney-General had had no scientific training but he had gained a passing knowledge during his long career. Solvents rather than water would have proved the particles to be what they unquestionably were, blood. It would have been impossible to take up the samples without taking metal scrapings at the same time. And of course those minute metal pieces would have rusted, submerged, as the man had conceded, for nearly a day in water. Once he had identified carbonate of iron, the idiot had considered his search over.

Flood frowned, hunched over his papers. Had he not kept Patron's examination absolutely secret, Flood would have suspected him of collusion with either Winchester or Morehouse and accused him of something far graver than incompetence.

He sighed. A realist, he accepted that nothing was to be achieved by recrimination. The evidence – the damning, clinching evidence which he had this day intended to announce to the enquiry and shatter all these carefully rehearsed accounts of derelict ships on the high seas – had been destroyed. It merely made his job harder; harder, but not impossible.

He shifted his attention, to where a scrap of cloth at the top of his bench covered against casual examination the exhibits he intended introducing. The now useless sword was there; and something else, which might have as upsetting an effect upon today's witness as he had hoped the weapon would do.

His gaze continued on to where Oliver Deveau, first mate of the *Dei Gratia*, was moving to the end of his evidence-in-chief, guided by the lawyer Pisani. Without the positive identification of blood, which would have shown the man's evidence to be nothing more than perjury, there was only one course left open to Flood. By the expertise and cleverness of his cross-examination he would have to make the court aware of the utter impossibility of what the *Dei Gratia* crew were claiming. And if such an admission could be obtained, this was the man from whom it should come. By his own evidence, Deveau had conceded that it had been he who first stepped aboard the *Mary Celeste* on December 5. If heinous work had been done that day, then Deveau had been actively involved.

No one *had* noticed his slight lessening in confidence, realised Flood, as Pisani sat down and Cochrane invited him to take up the questioning. Deveau was clearly ill at ease; more frightened than Morehouse had been the previous day. Occasionally the man's hand strayed up to his beard in a vague, combing motion and he felt his hair several times, as if assuring himself that it was not disarranged.

The inability to attack immediately with positive proof of bloodstaining was monstrous, decided Flood, as he stood up. It would have caused the witness's immediate collapse.

'It was a little after three o'clock in the afternoon when you set out for what you believed to be an abandoned vessel?' said Flood.

'Yes, sir.'

'What were the sea conditions?'

'There was a tolerably heavy sea running.'

'Describe how you first saw the *Mary Celeste*.'

Deveau hesitated, composing his recollection. 'Her head was westward when we first saw her. She was on starboard tack. With her foresail set, she would come up to the wind and fall off again. The wind was north, not much then, though blowing heavily in the morning. With the sails she had when I first saw her, she might come up and fall away a little, but not much. She would always keep those sails full. The sheet was fast on the port side. She was found on the starboard tack.'

'So from a rowing boat you had to board a vessel under sail in some wind.'

'Yes, sir.'

'Is it easy to do such a thing, unless the crew of the sailed vessel heaves to?'

Deveau frowned. 'There was no one aboard the *Mary Celeste*, sir,' he said, as if he thought the Attorney-General had misunderstood his earlier evidence.

'Exactly,' said Flood. 'So I will repeat the question. Is it not difficult to close to a sailed vessel in a rowing boat and then board?'

'The wind had slackened, as I said. The *Mary Celeste* had virtually no way on when we crossed to her.'

'So by the strength of your arms, you were able to row over and get aboard?'

The disbelief was pitched perfectly in Flood's voice.

'Yes, sir.'

Flood said nothing, letting the silence build up as if he expected Deveau to continue.

'How many of you were there in this rowing boat?' demanded Flood, when he considered Deveau sufficiently uncomfortable.

Before Deveau could respond, Pisani was on his feet, addressing the judge.

'Can there be any purpose whatsoever,' he said, 'in going point by point over everything that this man has already recounted in great detail and clarity in his evidence-in-chief, protracting this enquiry far beyond the time necessary?'

'I shall decide the time necessary for the conduct of this hearing, Mr Pisani,' rebutted Cochrane immediately. 'What need is there for haste?'

'I was not urging haste, sir,' said Pisani, aware he had antagonised the judge by a badly worded protest. 'I was suggesting that the time of this enquiry is being wilfully wasted.'

'Mr Attorney-General?' Cochrane asked.

Flood half-turned, away from Deveau and towards Pisani.

'My learned friend seems anxious for a conclusion,' he said, 'whereas I am anxious for the truth. Fractious for him though the search may be, I can only plead for his patience.'

Pisani refused to be overwhelmed by the sarcasm.

'Like my learned friend,' he said, 'I, too, am anxious that we should arrive at the truth of the matter. And I am equally anxious that it should be the *real* truth and that it will not be obscured for reasons that some of us present find difficult to comprehend.'

'I am experiencing no difficulty in comprehending the Attorney-General's questioning,' intruded Cochrane.

'Nor I, sir,' said Pisani immediately. 'It's the point of such questioning that is perhaps a little more difficult to ascertain.'

'Then I must repeat what I said to my learned friend not five minutes ago,' said Flood. 'If he has patience, then it all may become clear.'

'In which case,' intervened the judge again, anxious to end the dispute between the two advocates, 'I think we should continue.'

Flood came back to Deveau, aware that because of his interruption the man had had the opportunity to regain his composure.

'You were about to tell us the complement of the initial boarding party?' he reminded the witness.

'Seaman Johnson held the boat alongside,' said Deveau. 'I went aboard with second mate Wright.'

'What did you find?'

'There was much disarray,' said the man. 'There were lines and rigging over the deck and hanging over the rail. I tested the pumps and found three and a half feet of water. There was also a great deal of water below decks.'

'Was this the first thing you did?'

'Sir?'

'Commence an immediate examination of the *condition* of the vessel?' said Flood.

Deveau frowned, aware of a mistake and trying to realise what it was.

'Yes,' he said doubtfully.

'You knew from the moment of stepping over the rail, then, that there was no one aboard. Ill or incarcerated below decks, for instance?'

Colour spread from the man's neck and then up to his face.

'We had watched the ship for some hours through the glass,'

he said. 'There had never been any movement on deck in all that time.'

'*Below* deck, I said, Mr Deveau.'

'We shouted, of course. Before boarding. Asked permission to board, as is the custom. And then hulloed again, as soon as we were aboard.'

'Did you, Mr Deveau?'

Again the man hesitated, unable to see the Attorney-General's point.

'Or is that something you have just decided to add to your evidence at this moment?' pursued Flood.

'No, sir!' protested Deveau plaintively. 'It is as I said.'

'You initially conveyed the impression that you boarded the vessel without any attempt to discover whether there were people on board ... as if you knew the situation you were about to find.'

'That was the whole purpose of boarding, to render any assistance that was necessary. We had shouted from the *Dei Gratia* for almost an hour.'

Judging that the degree of doubt at the man's evidence had been sufficiently established, Flood said, 'Go on with what you found – after shouting loudly, that is.'

'I went first to the cabins, it being the most obvious place, I thought, to find if anybody were still aboard –'

'But there wasn't?'

'No, sir. The main cabin, which was slightly raised above the deck, was wet. Its door was open and its skylight raised. The windows on the starboard side were nailed up with planks and canvas and those on the port side shut.'

'Was the cabin in disarray?'

'Sir?'

'You've given evidence that there was some confusion and mess upon the deck. Was there anything in the main cabin that surprised you ... evidence that might have been produced, for instance, in a struggle?'

'Not a struggle, sir,' said Deveau doubtfully.

'What then?'

'I gained the impression that everything had been left behind in a great hurry.'

'A panic?'

'Great hurry,' repeated Deveau, refusing the other man's words.

'What had been left behind in this great hurry?'

'In the main cabin, I found charts, books and the slate-log which had been entered up to November 25 and showed that the vessel had made the island of Santa Maria. In some chests I found articles of women's clothing from which I assumed there had been a female aboard. Upon a pillow and some bedding in a bunk I saw what I thought was clearly the impression of where a child had lain.'

'A child?'

'Yes, sir. There was an outline most clearly marked. A small child, little more than a baby. In the cabin there were also some toys and a child's clothing ... dresses, things like that.'

'The bed was unmade?'

'Yes, sir. As I said, everything had the appearance of being hastily left. It was wet, too. I thought that was because of rain or squally weather coming in through the fanlight.'

'What else did you find?'

'There were two boxes, containing both men's and women's clothing. There was a work bag, containing needles, threads and buttons. And some books, all of a religious nature. There was a case of plotting instruments, a writing desk, a dressing case, some dirty clothes in a bag, a clock which had stopped, a sewing machine under a sofa and a rosewood harmonium or melodeon beneath the fanlight. Because of its positioning, it had got wet.'

Remembering how a long silence had upset the man before Pisani's intervention, Flood stood for several moments without putting another question. Deveau began shifting, gazing towards the *Dei Gratia* lawyer and then beyond, to where Captain Morehouse sat in the well of the court.

'Surely you discovered something else?' said Flood finally. 'Something more out of keeping than those articles about which you have spoken so far?'

'Sir?'

'What did you come upon beneath the captain's bunk?'

Deveau's face cleared.

'A sword,' he said.

From beneath the covering, the Attorney-General took the weapon in its scabbard and held it aloft. This had been the moment, he thought, when he could have produced the incontrovertible evidence of the fool Patron.

'This sword?' he said.

'Yes, sir.'

'Why did I have to prompt you about its finding?'

'Sir?'

'You appeared to have forgotten it.'

'You confused me by saying it was out of keeping with everything else,' said the man.

'You weren't surprised to find such a thing beneath a bunk!'

'No, sir.'

'A sword, Mr Deveau! Does your own captain arm himself in such a manner?'

'I did not regard it as a weapon.'

'Not a weapon! Really, Mr Deveau, you are straining the incredulity of this court. What is a sword, if it is not a weapon?'

'I thought of it as nothing more than a souvenir that the master of the vessel had obtained during his travels somewhere and put out of mind beneath his bunk.'

'Out of mind?'

'Yes, sir. It did not appear to have been put there with any care.'

'Thrust there for concealment, perhaps?'

'My impression was rather that it had just been put there ... a convenient storage place.'

Again Flood allowed the silence, to show the disbelief.

'What did you do with the sword?'

'Do, sir?'

'Didn't you examine it?'

'I believe I half-pulled it from its case ... I can't rightly recall.'

'You can't rightly recall, Mr Deveau?'

'I have said, sir, that I did not attach over-much importance to it. I believe I might have half-taken it out.'

'Why?'

Deveau shrugged. 'It's a sort of instinctive action, with a sword, isn't it?'

'I would not know. Perhaps you are better versed in the instinctive uses of swords than most people at this enquiry. Did you examine it, having extracted it?'

'I believe I looked at it ... ' The man's head was bent, in a genuine effort for recollection. He looked up, hopefully: 'I *did* look at it,' he said. 'I remember thinking it was of ornate design, the sort of thing one sees in Italy. There's a kind of crest upon the hilt.'

'The Cross of Savoy, I believe,' prompted Flood.

'I was unaware of what it was, sir. I thought of it only as a design.'

'So we have established that you did examine the sword. Tell this enquiry what you discovered.'

'Nothing,' said Deveau immediately.

'Nothing! We'll have a little more attention to detail than that, Mr Deveau. I'll repeat the question. What did you find upon the blade of the weapon?'

'Nothing that occurs to my memory now.'

Flood shifted irritably. The man was more obtuse than clever, he decided.

'Were there not stains upon the blade?'

'I believe there were some marks. Rust, I took them to be.'

'Was it not really *stains*, Mr Deveau? Stains of blood, which had been hastily wiped?'

'I have said that almost everything in the cabin was very wet. I took the marks to be rust, caused by the sword becoming damp.'

'Were the marks positive spotting, as happens when metal commences to rust?'

'Not exactly, sir.'

Flood felt the stir of excitement. It was coming, he thought. Very slowly. But he was extracting the evidence he wanted. He would have to be careful his accent didn't begin overwhelming him, making the words difficult to comprehend:

'Explain *exactly* what they were?'

Deveau hesitated, seeking the words.

'Smeared,' he conceded finally.

'Does rust smear?'

'I considered it was rust recently forming ... that I caused the effect by withdrawing the blade from its scabbard.'

'Isn't the real explanation that it was not rust at all?' demanded Flood suddenly. 'Isn't the real explanation that it was unquestionably blood that had been hastily wiped after some horrific attack upon the captain and his family aboard the *Mary Celeste*?'

Flood had expected Deveau to react in confusion, but instead the man stood regarding him curiously.

'I know nothing of that, sir,' he said.

'Don't you, Mr Deveau?' Flood extended his hand, as if offering the sword he still held towards the man. 'Don't *you* know how these suspicious stains came to be upon this weapon?'

Deveau frowned again, this time with the growing awareness of what Flood was suggesting.

'No, sir,' he said anxiously. 'As God is my witness, I do not.'

'Alas,' said Flood, 'God appears to have absented himself that day from the side of Captain Briggs and his unfortunate family. Let's proceed with what else you found.'

'After the captain's cabin, we went to the galley,' took up the witness. 'The door was open. There was about a foot of water there, where the sea had come in. The stove was knocked out of place and the cooking utensils scattered everywhere –'

'As might have happened had there been an altercation ... a fight perhaps?' intruded Flood.

'I thought it the effect of the ship being tossed about by the weather. That and perhaps the sea flooding in.'

'There was no evidence of victuals, indicating a meal?'

'None.'

'Was the stove hot?'

'No. Quite cold and shifted, as I say.'

'What about the fo'c'sle?'

'There was great confusion in the seamen's quarters,' remembered Deveau. 'I found the men's oilskins, boots and even their pipes scattered about the place.'

'You have a great experience of sailing?'

'Since a boy of fifteen.'

'Tell me, what do you imagine would cause men to abandon a ship, as is being suggested by some witnesses that this vessel was abandoned, in such haste that qualified, trained seamen would not think to snatch up their boots, oilskins or even their pipes?'

'I do not know, sir.'

'Would you have expected people to leave the vessel in such unpreparedness?'

'No, I would not.'

87

'Yet, according to what you found in their quarters, this is exactly what happened?'

'Yes, sir.'

'I would now invite you to recall the conditions that existed on deck,' said Flood. He might have lost the initiative with the bloodstains through the incompetence of the analyst, but his other prime exhibit was going to be more difficult to explain away.

'The main hatch was securely fastened and there were fenders upon which a boat had obviously been kept. The forehatch was off, though. So was the lazarette hatch, where the provisions and spare gear is stowed in the rear of the vessel. The water casks on deck had been moved, as if by heavy seas. The binnacle was stove-in and on its side, the compass destroyed. The stove pipe to the galley had been knocked over, I thought by the collapsed main staysail that was partially upon the galley roof. And as we had observed through the glass before boarding, the wheel was not lashed.'

'What about the rail?' began Flood.

'The rail?' queried Deveau cautiously.

'The rail, Mr Deveau ...'

Theatrically, Flood took away the cloth, to disclose a section of the rail that he had had Vecchio remove from the impounded vessel.

'This rail,' he said, holding it up and then gesturing for Vecchio to take it from him and carry it to the witness.

'Examine it,' he demanded.

Deveau took the exhibit and stared down at it.

'What is that half-way along that rail section?' demanded Flood.

'A cut, sir.'

'A cut, sir,' parroted Flood confidently. 'Is it not a very sharp cut? And deep? The sort of mark that it would have needed a particularly sharp weapon ... an axe, for instance ... to inflict?'

'Yes.'

'During your examination of the deck area, what cause did you conclude for this mark?'

'I did not see it.'

'Not see it, Mr Deveau! Is it not obvious enough and deep enough for anyone seeking an explanation for the mystery of the

Mary Celeste, the very function for which you had crossed to the vessel, to seize upon immediately?'

'It is deep, certainly.'

'Would you have expected to have seen it, from your examination?'

'Yes.'

'But you didn't?'

'No.'

'Why would that be?'

'I do not know.'

'Is it not yet another indication, along with everything else you have told us during your evidence, pointing to there having been aboard this vessel a most violent fracas?'

'I would not like to guess how the mark came to be upon the rail.'

'Why not?' said Flood.

'Because there is no way of my knowing.'

'Isn't there, Mr Deveau? Isn't there a way you could help this court about this injury, were you so minded?'

To his right, Pisani rose, his chair grating noisily and on purpose across the floor.

'Sir,' he said, to the judge. 'Surely this questioning amounts to nothing more than irrational, unnecessary harassment? Mr Deveau is making every effort to assist, to be met on all quarters by innuendo.'

Slowly Sir James Cochrane came up from the ledger into which he had been writing his own notes of the evidence.

He indicated the book, then said, 'I am assembling the most careful notation of the evidence. And so far it occurs to me that the Attorney-General is engaged not so much in innuendo as in a genuine effort to ascertain whatever truth might lie at the bottom of this incident.'

There was more noise, again caused purposely, as Pisani slumped back reluctantly into his chair.

'Proceed, Mr Flood,' Cochrane invited him.

'Could the damage to the rail have been caused by you or your men?' said Flood.

Deveau shook his head, more a gesture of helplessness than denial. When he spoke, it was obvious that he had realised in advance the danger of losing control and was making a conscious effort to remain composed under Flood's interrogation:

'I do not think it was caused by the men I eventually took with me to form a salvage crew.'

'Or prior to your forming a salvage crew?'

'I saw no one with an axe in hand. There was no cause.'

'Really, Mr Deveau?' said Flood suspiciously. He had succeeded well in casting doubt upon the man's evidence, the Attorney-General decided.

'No one in my presence ever carried an axe, nor inflicted the damage upon this rail.'

'What about the blood?' said Flood. He was hurrying the questioning now, in an effort further to shake the other man's composure.

'I do not know what you mean,' said Deveau.

'Wasn't there blood upon the deck?'

'I saw none.'

'There will be subsequent witnesses to yourself who will attest that there were clearly signs of blood, even after the *Mary Celeste* berthed here.'

'I saw none,' repeated Deveau stubbornly.

'After you and your salvage crew took control, did you wash the decks?'

'No, sir.'

'Or scrape them?'

'No, sir. We did not have enough men for that. We had to concentrate upon the sailing.'

'What, then, would be your reaction to knowing that a trained surveyor who is later to give us the benefit of his expert knowledge will declare that in his opinion the decks had been washed?'

Deveau was perspiring freely, his hands moving nervously in front of him.

'I can only repeat that there was no active washing or scraping when I was in command. Of course, during the time it took us to reach Gibraltar, the decks would have been awash from the sea.'

'Awash from the sea,' said Flood, isolating the evidence for fresh disbelief.

'What about boats?' he asked suddenly, urging the man on.

'There were no boats. Through the stern davits there was a

spar, from which I inferred she had not carried a boat there; when there is no boat on the stern davits, it is the custom to keep them steady by lashing through a spar.'

'Where would she have carried her boat then?'

'It was possible to see where the boat had been lashed across the main hatch. There were no lashings remaining. Nor was there any block or tackle, to show that she had been launched that way.'

'How, then, would a boat be got into the water?'

'The crew could have manhandled her over the rail. I do not think it would have been a difficult thing to do.'

'Why would a boat have been launched in this way?'

'The need to quit the vessel in a hurry.'

'Apart from the disarray in which you say you found things, was the *Mary Celeste* seaworthy?'

'Completely so.'

'More so than a lifeboat?'

'Of course,' said Deveau, as if the question were ridiculous.

'What, then, would have caused an experienced captain and crew to hurl their boat over the rail, without bothering with block and tackle, abandoning a seaworthy craft for something less safe?'

'There must have been a sudden panic.'

'A panic sufficient for the seamen to flee without boots, oilskins or pipes?'

'That must be the conclusion,' said Deveau, his discomfort growing.

'Captain Briggs, so fond of his family that he even took them upon voyage with him, must have been severely panicked to risk the life of a small child in an open boat, mustn't he?'

'That must be the presumption.'

'Mustn't it also be the presumption that the only thing which would have caused such panic would be terror ... the sort of terror, for instance, that would have been inculcated by a boarding party carrying axes and wielding swords ... ?'

'I must protest!' erupted Pisani, rising from his bench. 'This is not questioning ... it's hypothesis of the most outrageous kind. How can this witness possibly assist with such speculation?'

Cochrane nodded, looking almost regretfully towards the Attorney-General.

'I am as determined as you, Mr Flood, to discover the circumstances of this apparent tragedy,' he said. 'But I think there could be a little more moderation in the examination.'

Flood twitched his head in bird-like acknowledgment of the rebuke, keeping the annoyance from his face.

'Tell us of the rigging,' he said shortly.

'It was in very bad order,' said the witness. 'The standing rigging was all right. The fore-topsail and upper fore-topsail were gone, I think blown from the yards. The lower fore-topsail was hanging by its four corners. The main staysail was hauled down and lying loose on the galley and forward hatch, as if it had been collapsed. The jib and fore-topsail were set. All the other sails were furled. The rigging on the port side was broken. The starboard lower topsail brace was broken, the main peak halyard was broken and the gear of the foresail all broken.'

'How do you imagine this damage came about?'

'The only explanation must be that she had been cast about for a considerable time without anyone to man her or properly trim her sails.'

'Cast about, without anyone to trim her sails,' repeated Flood. 'Yet when you discovered her, the *Mary Celeste* although sailing back upon herself, was pursuing the course to be expected for her destination. Isn't that strange?'

'Yes, sir, it is.'

'Inexplicable, in fact?'

'I suppose so.'

'What explanation do you advance, for such a thing?'

'I can't, sir.'

'Any more than you can account for the axe slash to the deck rail or the bloodstaining to the sword blade or the evidence which must surely indicate a most violent fracas?'

'No, sir.'

'I have a question to put to you ... perhaps the most important of this whole examination and I want you to consider it fully before attempting to answer ... '

He paused. He could sense the apprehension in the other man.

'I must ask you whether the evidence you have given this enquiry is as complete as it could be. Is there nothing you feel able to volunteer that could help this enquiry to arrive at the solution of this mystery?'

92

Flood glanced towards the advocates' bench, half-expecting another protest from Pisani, but the lawyer representing the salvors remained seated. Even so, Deveau responded quicker than Flood had expected.

'I have told this enquiry everything that I honestly felt would help,' he said.

'Honestly?' picked up Flood, seizing the word.

'Yes, sir,' said Deveau defiantly. 'Absolutely honestly.'

'Were there not men aboard the *Mary Celeste* when you came upon her, men whom you expected to encounter?'

Deveau frowned, in apparent confusion.

'I've told you the ship was abandoned … deserted – '

'And I am asking you if that is true.'

'Yes, sir!'

'You are the first mate of the *Dei Gratia*?'

'Yes.'

'But Captain Morehouse permitted you the captaincy of the salvage crew?'

'Although sailing as a first mate, I have obtained my master's certificate.'

Flood smiled, as if the answer were illuminating.

'So you will shortly seek a captaincy?'

'That is, of course, my ambition.'

'Would money assist that ambition?'

'Money?'

'Yes, sir. Money,' repeated Flood. 'Money which would be useful in some share purchase, for instance in a ship-owning firm?'

'I have not considered such a course,' said Deveau.

'It is your hope, is it not, to receive a substantial award for the salvage of the *Mary Celeste*?'

'I seek what the enquiry considers I have earned in bringing this vessel, laden with a cargo still dischargeable, to a port of safety,' said Deveau formally.

Flood stood quite unmoving and did not speak for several moments.

Finally he said, 'I wonder, Mr Deveau, what the view of this enquiry will be about the just reward for what you did regarding the *Mary Celeste*?'

Deveau made as if to speak, but Flood went on, preventing him:

'Having concluded my cross-examination of this witness for the time being, I seek permission to recall Captain Winchester ... '

Captain Winchester would have long ago realised that the earlier impression of unpreparedness was a courtroom trick, so Flood abandoned that demeanour. He began instead with an immediate forcefulness that he calculated would jar the ship-owner:

'You knew Captain Morehouse?'

'Through the letter of introduction sent me by Captain Briggs I have made his acquaintance.'

'How did the character of Captain Morehouse impress itself upon you?'

'Captain Briggs described him in his letter to me as an excellent mariner, a first-class sailor. My initial impression was that it was a good assessment.'

'You liked him?'

'Yes.'

'And determined to find a position for him?'

'Our discussion did not reach such a stage.'

'What stage did it reach, Captain Winchester?'

The ship-owner shrugged. 'Like most first interviews, little more than the establishing of contact.'

'Just the establishing of contact,' repeated Flood. 'No discussion of how finance might be raised, to enable the admittedly ambitious Captain Morehouse to attain his own vessel?'

'No.'

'No discussion of any money at all?'

'Only of the most general character ... the stating of the obvious, that were he to enter into any situation of partnership, then he would need capital for a share issue.'

There was none of the condescension of his first period of evidence about the American this time, the Attorney-General decided. Winchester was tensed and alert, aware that his account was disbelieved and anxious to avoid any mistakes.

'Did you like him better than Captain Briggs?'

'Such a comparison never occurred to me.'

'How did your discussion end, on this first occasion?'

'With my agreeing to see Captain Morehouse when he returned from his voyage to Gibraltar.'

'Why?'

'I'm sorry,' said Winchester, 'I don't understand the question.'

'What was so important about the voyage to Gibraltar?'

Winchester extended his hands, still indicating lack of comprehension.

'Nothing,' he said. 'Who suggested there was?'

'The decision to meet after the conclusion of the current voyage had about it nothing of a test for Captain Morehouse ... for you to obtain some indication of his determination for captaincy?'

'This is the most preposterous innuendo,' interrupted Cornwell, lurching up in protest from the lawyers' bench. 'There must be a limit to what is admissible in this court, surely?'

Cochrane looked irritably at the lawyer, then at the Attorney-General. The irritation, realised Flood, was that the judge had to agree with the objection.

'I think we might contain ourselves a little more to the point, Mr Flood,' he said, making the admonition as gentle as possible.

The Attorney-General lowered his head in acceptance, almost a pecking gesture, then went back to Winchester.

'I am struck by an oddness about what I have heard at this enquiry,' he began quietly. 'During your evidence to this court, you imagine a sword discovered beneath Captain Briggs's bunk to be a souvenir and hazard a guess that some bizarre freak weather condition caused the abandonment of the *Mary Celeste*. Bad weather is the explanation from Captain Morehouse for whatever occurred near the Azores ... And also of the chief mate Deveau, whom we heard this morning also suggest that the sword was a casually bought memento of a previous voyage ... '

He paused, building to his point.

'Sitting here, day after day, listening as carefully as I have, I have been struck by the similarity of view expressed by everyone so far ... a similarity which almost indicates a rehearsal —'

Winchester stood at the witness stand, alternately gripping and ungripping the rail at the top of the carved surround. Fear? wondered Flood. Or anger?

'I protest to this hearing against the type of questioning to which I am being subjected,' the owner burst out. 'Captain Briggs was a man I liked and respected. As I made clear when I first gave evidence, I regarded him as someone with whom I was proud to be associated. I consider as the most outrageous calumny the attempt being made at this enquiry to make it appear that I was in some way involved in collusion to do away with the captain and crew for some paltry sum that could be claimed against insurance for the salvage of the vessel … '

He halted, out of breath and words, staring at the Attorney-General as if demanding a challenge. A much-worried man, judged Flood.

'So the fact that three witnesses at this enquiry all offer the same conclusion is nothing more than coincidence?' said Flood.

Winchester tried to answer, but the Attorney-General refused him, wanting to drive the accusation home.

'Yet another coincidence,' he said. 'Like that of the abandoned *Mary Celeste* being found by the very man who had dined with Captain Briggs the night before her New York sailing … yet another coincidence, like the derelict, drifting vessel being on course for the passage she was supposed to be keeping?'

Winchester made a gesture of weariness:

'I do not consider it surprising that three witnesses come independently to the same view of the cause of the tragedy. We have all of us had a long and varied experience of the sea. From that experience, some unknown weather condition *must* be the likeliest explanation.'

'So you and everyone else from whom we have heard so far are at great pains to have this enquiry believe,' said Flood.

'It is as logical and more based upon likelihood than those which you have so far attempted to advance,' said Winchester irritably.

'A decision not to be made by you, Captain Winchester, but by a judge far more versed in selecting truth from falsehoods than any other man here today … '

He paused, imagining that Winchester was about to say something and wanting to give the man every opportunity to overreach and hopefully condemn himself from his own mouth. But the American ship-owner appeared to change his mind, lowering his head and avoiding the Attorney-General's examination.

'Do you ever expect to see Captain Briggs, his family or any of the *Mary Celeste* crew alive again?' said Flood suddenly.

'Sir?' frowned Winchester.

'From the witness Deveau you have heard this morning that a boat was missing from the deck, indicating some escape. Do you think it is possible someone at least might still be rescued?'

'I suppose it is a possibility,' conceded Winchester.

'I detect a note of doubt in your attitude.'

'Were there to be survivors from whatever happened, I would have expected word of them by now. The *Mary Celeste* was sailing a much-used route.'

'So you've personally little hope?'

'Sadly, no.'

'Sadly, Captain Winchester?'

'Of course,' said the owner immediately, his renewed anger obvious.

'I wonder, Captain Winchester, if there were survivors found even at this late stage and they were able to give evidence before this enquiry, what account they would give of what happened?'

The American took his time with the answer, belatedly recognising the futility of temper:

'Whatever it might be, I am sure the solution would be far different from that which you are attempting to thrust upon this hearing,' he said.

Because it was closest to the enquiry chamber, Consul Sprague's house had continued to be the venue for the daily meetings after the court had risen.

Inevitably it was Winchester who assumed the role of chairman, better able among those who sympathised to express his outrage.

'Anyone any doubts left now?' he said, hunched forward in his chair.

'He's determined upon a conspiracy,' agreed Captain Morehouse, who had become part of the group.

'With me the centre of it,' protested the owner.

'And me the agent,' said Morehouse, feeling as powerless as the other man.

'I've attempted a private meeting with the judge,' said Sprague, aware that his conduct as American Consul might be questioned if these men complained to Washington. 'I've received a formal note telling me that it would be improper for there to be any discussion between us in chambers until the conclusion of the hearing.'

'I'll not be railroaded,' insisted Winchester, mouthing the familiar determination more to himself than to the others in the room. 'I'm damned if I'll just sit around and become enmeshed in whatever conclusion that confounded man is intent upon.'

'He's made good use of the circumstantial evidence,' said the cargo owners' lawyer, Martin Stokes, in reluctant praise.

'But that's all it is,' argued Pisani. 'Completely circumstantial, without a shred of anything positive to prove the crime upon which he's obviously intent.'

'That axe mark was evidence, surely?' disputed Cornwell. 'Sailors don't go around slashing their own vessels.'

'There's no proof it's an axe mark,' said Winchester, irritated now at the lawyers' attitude. 'It's just obvious that the rail has been cut, nothing more. There's certainly no proof that the mark came from the blade of an axe.'

'Let's not get embroiled again in hypothesis,' protested Cornwell. He looked directly at Winchester and Morehouse.

'It doesn't look good for either of you,' he said honestly.

'What the hell are Washington doing about it all?' the owner demanded of Sprague. 'Isn't your function here to protect American citizens?'

The Consul had been afraid of such an open question.

'I've been asked by the Secretary of the Treasury to provide daily transcripts of the evidence,' he said.

'And?' persisted Winchester.

Sprague, shifted, embarrassed.

'There has been nothing official, of course,' he said, 'but I get the impression from some of the communications I am receiving that they seem to accept the belief of the Attorney-General.'

'What!' exclaimed Winchester.

Sprague nodded. 'They seem to believe some sort of crime has been committed.'

'Oh my God,' said Winchester softly.

8

A wave, unseen but big to judge by the effect it had, twisted into the side of the *Mary Celeste* and the whole vessel shuddered into a crab-like slide before the man at the wheel corrected, righting her on course again. Captain Briggs, who had almost completed the log, looked down at the near-finished entry, then added, 'Squally, rising frequently to gales.'

He closed the book, sitting back. It had been a rough voyage. Not the worst he had ever known. But rough, nevertheless. As if in confirmation of this thoughts, the ship pitched into a trough, stretching the timbers, which creaked and strained around him. The log slid away, coming to rest against the protective fender which edged his desk, and the lamp rocked on its pivots.

There would be no need to check for damage. Days before he had given the order to batten down and secure everything movable and by now he was sufficiently confident of the crew to know that the instructions had been obeyed to the letter. Not even the deckhouse planking or pitch caulking had been cracked by the sea, so well was the ship being handled. The galley was the only area where things might have been lying loose, but the cook-steward, William Head, had proved himself as good a seaman as he was a victualler. Briggs decided he might enquire about the galley later; it would show the sort of consideration that the men appreciated.

There was another sound, like a sudden hammering, and Briggs realised they had been swamped by a wave. Momentarily the vessel seemed to squat in the water, then there was a visible sensation of her rising again. It was nothing to worry about, he knew. A less seaworthy vessel would be taking more water than the *Mary Celeste*, although even she was certainly awash, as she had been ever since the voyage began.

At first he had expected it, having the pumps checked sometimes as frequently as every hour. When they had registered no more than an inch averaged over a twenty-four-hour period he had suspected them of malfunctioning, even having Arien Martens strip one down, to check. But the pumps were in perfect working order; just as the *Mary Celeste* was in perfect sailing order. He looked around the cabin, self-conscious in his admiration. His proprietorial expression, Sarah called it. Briggs was aware that his feelings went far beyond any pride of ownership. It was a seaman's appreciation of a good ship, the emotion he would have known even if he had had no part in her.

Whatever doubts he might have had about his investment those last few days before leaving New York had been blown away by the gales they had encountered daily. The *Mary Celeste* had behaved magnificently, worked by a crew who had come up to his highest expectations. Once they entered the Mediterranean, it would become more like a pleasure cruise than a working voyage; with luck, the weather might improve before they passed the Straits of Gibraltar.

He turned as his wife came from the child's sleeping area:

'How is she?'

'Asleep, for the moment. She's exhausted.'

Sarah's face was pinched with fatigue and worry. Sophia's seasickness had begun almost from the time they had left the Staten Island anchorage and worsened with every day. Only in the last twenty-four hours had they managed to get her to take the porridge which the cook had had constantly ready, hoping for an improvement, and so for several days the baby had been retching on an empty stomach and Sarah had been fearful of some internal injury or strain.

'It should get better soon.'

'I've been hoping that for days,' said the woman.

There was another side wave, jarring the ship, and Sarah staggered. Briggs snatched out, supporting her.

'We are no more than three or four days' sailing from the Azores,' said Briggs. 'We're in the Gulf Stream already.'

'I thought I'd go out on deck for a moment, while she's resting. It's almost claustrophobic in here.'

So bad had the weather been that the child had only once used the brace that Arien Martens had constructed and then she had been thrown over by a sudden movement of the ship, bruising her arm. Martens had made a harness for Sarah's infrequent deck visits and she began fitting it into place over the top of her oilskins. Briggs helped her, ensuring that the ropes were properly secured, and then got into his own protective clothing.

The wind snatched at them immediately they opened the companion-way door, so forcefully that Sarah gasped as the breath was taken from her. Briggs got to windward of his wife, trying to shield her, arm around her shoulders as he guided her towards the safety rope stretched between the two masts. The vessel was on the shortest canvas, just topsail and jib, yet it was still heeled over, with the starboard rail awash. She clung to him, struggling to get a footing against the wet, sloping deck. He tethered the line from her harness to the safety rope, then cupped his mouth to her ear:

'Do you want me to remain with you?'

She shook her head, positively.

'Sure?'

There was another head shake, more of irritation this time. Sarah was always annoyed when his concern for her threatened any interference with his work.

Briggs clutched at the rope himself, grateful for the support as he made his way to the wheel. The fourth German member of the crew, Gottlieb Goodschall, was at the helm, a rope looped around his waist and tying him to a wheel brace.

At twenty-three, Goodschall was the youngest of the Germans and spoke the least English. He stood legs splayed, hands tight against the wheel spokes, forcing the vessel on course. He was drenched with spray, the water funnelling from the brim of his sou'wester and down the back of his oilskin cover.

Knowing conversation was almost impossible, Briggs nodded to the man, staring over his shoulder to determine the cause for the sideways buffeting. They had encountered a freak current, he recognised, seeing the build-up of the water, so that the sea was being driven in two directions. To stay windward, as they must to retain any control, meant that occasionally they were struck amidships by the current.

Such a wave came now and Briggs tensed himself against it,

turning to gesture to Sarah. She saw it in time, hauling herself in along her safety line and grabbing the larger rope before it hit the ship, head bent against the wall of spray-tipped water which spumed over the deck. Briggs stayed watching her until he saw that she had suffered no more than a wetting, then turned back to the helm. Aware that the captain had seen what was happening, the young German made to speak and Briggs bent close to him.

'Won't last,' said Goodschall, indicating the side current.

'Hope you're right,' said Briggs.

'Lessening this past hour,' the man assured him.

For the first time Briggs noticed that there were other crewmen on deck. The Lorensen brothers were to starboard, checking the ties on the furled sails. There was always a danger in such weather that the hastily secured sails might be ripped open and then either blown overboard or, worse, trail in the water to snarl the steering gear and even endanger the ship. Briggs had sailed in many vessels where the crew would have waited until the weather abated.

He moved on, to the fo'c'sle head. Richardson and the second mate, Andrew Gilling, were hunched in its protection.

'Helmsman says it's lessening,' said Briggs.

'About time,' said Gilling. His Danish parentage showed in his accent, despite the time he had lived in America.

'How's the baby?' asked Richardson. From the first mate's concern over the preceding week, it would have been easy to imagine the child was his.

'Took some porridge today. Now she's sleeping,' said Briggs. He indicated the brothers straddling the spars on the port side now.

'Seem to have nearly all the crew aloft,' he said. 'Shouldn't there be a watch in their bunks?'

'There's time enough for rest,' said Richardson. 'Better to ensure the ship safe.'

'Any damage?' Despite his conviction in the cabin, it was an instinctive question.

Richardson gestured to the bow of the vessel.

'Martens was checking the bowsprit and found some odd splintering.'

'Splintering?' said Briggs, immediately concerned.

'Not deep, as far as we can see,' reported Richardson, 'although

I'll be happier when this weather drops and we can maybe examine it from a boat. Runs for six or seven feet on either side and looks to be cut as clean as with a knife.'

'Either side?' queried Briggs. 'That's unusual.'

'I'm minded it's the corkscrewing caused by getting the sea on two quarters at once,' said Richardson. 'There's been a lot of strain on the timbers.'

'I'd have expected them to sustain it better than that, though.'

'Could have been faulty planking.'

'How close to the water?'

'High enough,' assured the first mate. 'When the sea comes down it'll be a good three to four feet above the waterline.'

'Checked for'ard leakage?' asked Briggs.

'None at all,' said Richardson.

'Let's examine it, at the first opportunity,' said Briggs.

'I'd like to get the hatches open, too,' said Richardson. 'Temperature has gone up since we got into the Gulf Stream. Must be three to four degrees' difference since we left New York.'

'How is it?' asked Briggs.

'Smelly,' said Richardson. 'I checked through the for'ard hatch.'

'Leaking then?'

'Almost inevitable, through red oak.'

'Breathable?'

'Yes,' said Richardson.

'So no immediate problem?'

'Still like to get some air circulating down there. It's unpredictable stuff.'

'No risk of any shifting?'

Richardson shook his head confidently. 'We double-lashed in New York,' he reminded the captain.

Briggs determined he would give Richardson the best report possible before the man signed off in New York on their return. There had been nothing about which he had had to correct or instruct the first mate since the commencement of the voyage.

'Goodschall was right.'

Briggs and Richardson turned away from the cover of the fo'c'sle, looking out to sea, as Gilling spoke. The squall was still high but the side waves had subsided.

'Should get even better, when we get into the lee of the Azores,' said Richardson.

'Still some way away,' warned Briggs.

'At least the worst is behind us,' said Gilling.

Because the wind was still high, they were too far away to hear the cry, but Sarah detected it, screaming out for her husband.

Briggs turned as the woman cried out again: 'Sophia. Something's happened to Sophia.'

She was hauling herself along on the safety line, slithering against the deck. Surer-footed, Briggs ran along the deck, so that he was beside his wife when they got to the companion-way. From the cabin came the sound of Sophia's screams.

Briggs went in first, stopping just inside the door. The child's nightdress was smeared with blood and there was more upon her cheek, pale from her constant sickness and therefore showing an almost unreal brightness.

'Dear God,' said Sarah, from behind.

It was only when he got nearer that Briggs saw the souvenir sword he had bought in Naples when he had commanded the schooner *Forest King*. The blade had been half withdrawn from the scabbard; while taking the sword out the baby had cut deeply into her thumb.

He snatched the weapon up as his wife took the child into her arms, cradling the tear-stained face into her breast.

For once Briggs's control went.

'Confounded thing!' he said angrily, hurling it away from them. It struck his bunk and then fell to the deck.

Richardson had followed them to the cabin door and had seen what had happened. Within minutes he was back with a first-aid kit, cupping the child's hand in his palm and carefully cleaning the wound with diluted spirit.

'It's not too bad,' he said. 'In a child this young, it won't even scar.'

As quickly as it had erupted, Briggs's anger began to subside.

'It was careless of me to leave it lying around in the cabin, where she could get to it,' he apologised to Sarah. 'I'm sorry.'

The woman smiled, her concern less now she could see the extent of the injury.

'It's nobody's fault,' she said.

'Better put it somewhere where she won't get it again,' said Richardson.

Briggs walked across to the weapon, hefting it in his hand. Quickly he opened the cupboard beneath the bunk and tossed it inside.

'She won't get it from there,' he said, testing the lock.

Thumb bound, Sophia nestled against her mother's chest and began to sleep again.

'Poor mite,' said Briggs. 'It'll be a long time before she wants to come to sea again.'

'See how quickly she's settled,' said Sarah. 'She feels so safe.'

The custom had arisen for Martens with his flute to accompany Mrs Briggs upon the melodeon, but because the weather had lessened and the child settled comfortably to sleep after another meal of William Head's porridge there had been no music that night in the captain's quarters.

Instead Martens had played a while for those members of the crew not on watch, finally putting the instrument aside and settling down with his pipe.

'I'm glad the child seems to be improving,' said Richardson. The crew had invited him to the fo'c'sle.

The German nodded. 'She reminds me of my own children,' he said.

'How long have you been away from Amrun?' asked the first mate.

'Maybe nine months,' said Martens.

'A long time.'

'The pay is better than piloting around Hamburg,' said Martens. 'But I miss them. I think I'll sign off in Gibraltar and get passage home.'

Richardson nodded. He expected that most of the Germans would do the same. It would mean selecting a new crew in the British colony and he doubted whether they would be as good as this one. He would have to discuss it with Captain Briggs. With his family aboard, it was natural he should be more than normally concerned at the quality of his crew.

'You any children?' asked Martens.

'Not yet,' said Richardson. 'Married less than eight months.'

'As much a strain being at sea, then,' said the German, 'with such a new wife.'

'Hope to get my own vessel when we get back to America,' said the first mate. 'Then she'll sail with me.'

The Lorensen brothers entered, overhearing the last part of the conversation.

'I'll not engage in long trips when I marry,' said Boz Lorensen.

'Maybe you'll come to regard it as a welcome relief,' joked his brother, who was four years older.

'Not with Ingrid,' said Boz confidently.

'When's the wedding?' said Martens.

'Three months,' said the other German. 'If you're ashore, I'd like you and your wife to come.'

'I didn't know you all came from the same town,' said Richardson.

'Hardly a town,' said Martens. 'It's a small village called Altersum, on the island of Föhr. I've moved to Amrun now, but most of my family remain.' He turned to Boz: 'I was just saying that I think I'll go home after this trip. So I'd like to come; it would be a good homecoming party.'

'I'm planning to make it so,' said Boz. 'By sailing deep-sea I've saved nearly $500.'

'Only by ensuring that I pay all the tobacco and victualling when we're between ships,' said Volkert, still joking.

If there were to be discussion with Captain Briggs about the crew, he might as well establish the intention of as many as possible, decided Richardson.

'You'll be signing off in Gibraltar then?' he said, expectantly.

The brothers exchanged looks.

'Depends how quickly a homeward cargo is found,' said Volkert, answering for both of them. 'If there were something immediate, there would still be time to return to New York, then cross to Europe again before Boz's wedding.'

'There's cargo waiting,' said Richardson.

'Then we'll probably stay,' said the elder brother. Richardson had become aware during the voyage that Volkert made the decisions for both of them.

'I might even be able to save $600,' said the younger man.

Richardson smiled, recognising for the first time the man's

feeling for money. It was a welcome parsimony, he thought. It would be far easier replacing only Martens in Gibraltar. And it would mean returning to New York with an excellent crew almost intact. He continued the thought. Captain Winchester had virtually promised him his own ship upon his return. He would set out on his first command a contented man if he could have aboard two men as tried and trusted as these brothers. If money were what they sought, they might welcome a short, well-paid coastal trip before shipping back to Europe.

'You talk as if you want to become a millionaire,' Martens said to Boz.

'I'm determined to be a rich man,' said the other German. 'I'll not let my wife live in poverty.'

'I wish you luck,' said Richardson, arrested by the man's seriousness.

'Boz believes he can make his own luck,' said Volkert, smiling to indicate that he didn't have the same conviction.

The Attorney-General decided he had been wrong in his assessment of the analyst's mistake. It had been irritating; profoundly so. But that was all. Certainly not disastrous, as he had first feared. By the ability with which he had inflicted doubt upon every testimony so far presented, he had preserved his case from any damage that might have been caused by his not being able to prove positive bloodstaining.

And he still had his own witnesses, whose evidence supported every contention he had so far advanced.

Flood slouched back in his chair, gazing at the witness stand. With the simple seamen who were now being called to support the evidence of the officers who had preceded them, he did not imagine he would have great difficulty in maintaining the court's suspicion.

John Wright, the second mate from the *Dei Gratia*, looked apprehensively across the chamber as Flood rose.

'You boarded the *Mary Celeste* with Mr Deveau?'

'Yes, sir.'

'And were therefore, with Mr Deveau, the first person aboard after whatever disaster befell the vessel?'

Wright considered his reply, knowing what had happened to the others and wanting to avoid mistakes. At last, he said, 'Yes, I suppose so.'

'And what do you suppose that disaster to be?'

The man's throat moved visibly and he seemed to make several attempts to speak.

'I don't know,' he said. 'As the rest have said ... bad weather.'

'Why as the rest have said? Weren't you able to form your own assessment? Or are we discussing the general story that seems to have been agreed upon before this enquiry began?'

'But it must have been something to do with the weather, mustn't it?'

'Must it? Would you abandon a perfectly seaworthy vessel for a lifeboat in bad weather?'

'Of course not,' said the man, as if his common sense were being impugned.

'Of course not,' said Flood. 'So once again we have disposed of this myth that some strange manifestation of climate caused nine sensible, sober adults to take a baby and cast themselves adrift in a small boat. So I will put the question to you again. What do you suppose happened?'

'Don't know,' said the man, aware that he was being manipulated, but unable to prevent it.

'You don't know! Are you telling this enquiry that since boarding a floating derelict in a salvage operation from which you hope to gain some substantial award, you have not put your mind to the question of what might have caused the vessel's abandonment?'

'Some panic,' said Wright. 'The things we found in the cabin meant they must have gone very quickly.'

'We've already disposed, by the use of simple logic, of the theory that it could have been the weather. So what do you suppose could have caused these experienced people to panic?'

'They were frightened.'

'Indeed they must have been frightened, but of what, do you imagine?'

'How can I say ... there was no way of knowing ... '

'So every member of the *Dei Gratia* crew who has so far given evidence has been quick to assure the enquiry,' said Flood. He held up the sword.

'Did you see this?'

'I was with Mr Deveau when he found it, in the captain's cabin.'

'Did you see the bloodstains?'

'I saw the blade was discoloured.'

'With bloodstains?' persisted Flood.

'I thought it was rust.'

'Because Mr Deveau said so.'

'I suppose so.'

'Could the discoloration have been blood?'

'I suppose so.'

'Let us try to become a little more positive, Mr Wright. Could the marks upon the blade have been blood, just as easily as they could have been rust?'

'Yes.'

Flood decided that the questioning was going far better than he had hoped; surely there could be no doubt of crime after today?

'What about this?' he said, taking the piece of rail from the bench. 'Did you see this?'

'No, sir.'

'Any more than Mr Deveau,' said Flood, in a sarcastic aside. He gestured to the court marshal, to carry it to the witness.

'What is that mark upon the wood?'

'It would seem to be some sort of cut.'

'A deep cut?'

'Yes.'

'What do you imagine would be necessary to cause such damage?'

'Something heavy,' said the man. 'An axe, perhaps.'

'Do sensible, experienced sailors go around slashing the rails of their vessels with an axe?'

Again the man frowned, imagining mockery.

'Of course not.'

'So how do you think it got there?'

'I don't know.'

'Don't you?'

'I said I don't.'

'Couldn't that damage have been caused during that moment of terror which caused the crew to abandon ship?'

'Perhaps ... I don't know.'

'What sort of panic and terror wields an axe?'

'I don't understand, sir,' protested the seaman.

'Has it ever occurred to you, since you came upon this allegedly abandoned vessel, that the *Mary Celeste* could have been taken over by a hostile crew?'

'Hostile? You mean pirates?'

'Just hostile. The Barbary Coast has been cleared of brigands these last fifty years.'

'But who … ' stumbled the man, and the Attorney-General took advantage of his incoherence:

'Who indeed! Can you help this enquiry with an answer to that question?'

'Me, sir!' said the witness, in surprise.

'You, sir,' said Flood.

The man gripped the edge of the stand, his shoulders humped in helplessness.

'But how?'

'You were the first over the rail, were you not? A rail upon which you failed to see an axe mark which we have agreed could have come about during a moment of terror.'

'The ship was deserted when we boarded,' said the seaman. 'There was nothing to tell us what had happened. Nothing at all – '

'So this enquiry has heard before,' sighed the Attorney-General. 'With an almost word-perfect repetition. How long deserted?'

'Many days, it must have been. When Mr Deveau tested the pumps, there was a lot of water. The cabins and galley were awash.'

'What about boats?'

'The davits at the stern were empty. I could not tell whether a boat had been launched from them or not. There was no indication, as far as I could see, whether there was accommodation for another boat on deck. I certainly saw no block and tackle to indicate that one had been launched from the deck.'

The Attorney-General began to prepare his final question, then paused, looking to the lawyers' benches. They had been strangely quiet today; perhaps confronted by the blatant inconsistencies in their clients' evidence they had at last accepted the futility of objections. He decided to rephrase the point he was about to make to the witness, anxious not to blur what he regarded as an excellent cross-examination by any belated, irritating interruption.

'You sailed from New York in the *Dei Gratia* on November 15?'

'Yes, sir.'

'And encountered the *Mary Celeste* on December 5?'

'Yes, sir.'

'And arrived here in Gibraltar on December 12?'

'Yes, sir.'

'Tell me, during those twenty-seven days did you at any time witness, or were you at any time involved in, any violent activity?'

Pisani at last stirred, about to rise, but before he could do so the seaman's anger broke.

'No!' he shouted across the enquiry chamber. 'I did nothing to harm anyone aboard the *Mary Celeste*.'

'You weren't asked if you had,' said Flood contentedly. 'But thank you for so openly expressing a thought which I am sure has occurred to many during the evidence we have heard so far.'

He sat quickly, still in advance of Pisani's intervention, leaving the crew's lawyer half out of his chair. Sir James Cochrane looked curiously towards him, but Pisani shook his head, lowering himself into his seat again.

Flood leaned forward over his bench, apparently concentrating upon his note-taking, as Charles Lund, a seaman who had been one of Deveau's salvage crew from the Azores to Gibraltar, was sworn in and began responding to Pisani's questions during his evidence-in-chief.

As a trained, practising lawyer, the Attorney-General had to recognise the evidence as circumstantial. But circumstantial or not, it was overwhelmingly that of crime. Either of mutiny and murder, with the connivance of the *Dei Gratia* crew with whom a high seas rendezvous had been arranged before the New York sailing, for the culprits to be aided by a safe landing somewhere along the coast of Spain. Or straight piracy by Captain Morehouse and his men.

There was something further he had to recognise. As well as being Attorney-General of the colony, he was also Admiralty Proctor, with responsibility to the Board of Trade in London.

And he would be grossly failing in that responsibility if, even in advance of any finding that Cochrane might return, he did not officially communicate his beliefs to London, for the authorities there to take whatever action they considered necessary. Mediterranean embassies and consulates in the area should be alerted for any sighting of the *Mary Celeste* crew, for instance. And Washington informed of the official view of affairs with far more force than he suspected Consul Sprague was attempting. With his constant pandering to the ship-owner and the *Dei Gratia* captain, Sprague showed himself too frightened of an adverse report about his personal conduct properly to carry out his duties.

It had been an onerous task, for which he had decided to give the man a bonus, but Flood had insisted upon his clerk's taking a verbatim transcript of the evidence. He decided that he would enclose copies of that transcript with his account to London, to enable the Board of Trade lawyers to consider the facts as fully as he had and arrive at their own verdict. The advantage of such a procedure would be to obtain the agreement of other legally trained minds.

The Attorney-General suddenly became aware that the court had turned to him and realised that he was being offered the chance to question Lund. Aware that he had not been concentrating upon the man's evidence, Flood's clerk pushed across a sheet of hastily written but nevertheless readable notes. For the first time, Flood saw, the crew lawyer had phrased his questions in anticipation of attack, trying to minimise any damaging cross-examination by obtaining denials of accusations before any had been made. The Attorney-General smiled, looking directly at Pisani. So they were becoming worried. And quite rightly so.

'You formed the second party to board the *Mary Celeste* ... the salvage crew?'

'Yes.'

'And were aboard for some seven to eight days?'

'Yes.'

The Attorney-General looked up from the clerk's notes, staring directly at the witness.

'Were you frightened?'

'Frightened?'

'Boarding a vessel you had found derelict at sea ... laying your head in quarters the last occupants of which had disappeared in such a mysterious way. Had contagion been aboard, for instance, you could have contracted it.'

'I am not a superstitious man,' said Lund. 'And I know of no illness that would have caused a complete abandonment of a vessel. There would have been bodies about.'

'There would indeed, sir. Unless the contagion was humanly inflicted. With the advantage you had of spending so much time aboard the *Mary Celeste*, were you able to discover anything which might assist this enquiry to a conclusion about what befell the people aboard?'

'No, sir.'

'Did you see the sword which Mr Deveau found?'

'No, sir.'

'Weren't you interested?'

'Not really. Mr Deveau thought nothing of it. The presence of such a souvenir is not unusual aboard ship.'

'Ah,' said the Attorney-General, as if suddenly enlightened. 'Evidence to which we have become so accustomed. You determined it a souvenir, along with all the others?'

'Yes.'

'The rigging was in disarray, we have heard?'

'Yes, sir. Some broken, more lying where the wind had cast it. The peak halyards were broken and gone.'

'Where the wind had cast them,' repeated Flood, to emphasise the remark. 'Did you encounter any evidence that something other than the wind might have caused this damage?'

'No, sir.'

'So positive! I must infer from that response that you suspected there might have been something else and that you made a special examination?'

'No. But we had to repair the rigging, before we could right the vessel and make towards Gibraltar. We were involved with the ropes nearly all of one day. Had they been cut, for instance, I'm sure I would have noticed. The others would, also.'

'But you didn't. And neither did they?'

'No.'

'How bad was the damage?'

'Considerable. There were sheets and braces hanging over both sides. As I said, the peak halyards were broken and gone.'

'I must put to you a question I have put to every witness so far, although I suspect I already know the answer. Having sailed in the *Mary Celeste* for the period you did and having come upon her in the condition you did, what conclusion did you reach as to the cause of her abandonment?'

'The weather, sir. It must have been the weather.'

'A response, Mr Lund, delivered with the spontaneity of a child learning its lessons by rote,' said the Attorney-General, sitting down.

It had been a good day, he decided. And tomorrow it would be better. Then he could start to introduce his own evidence, to assemble all the suspicions in the testimony of an accredited expert and then call others to support it. It would be interesting to see how Pisani and Cornwell and Stokes took it. And perhaps even more intriguing to witness the reaction of Captain Winchester and the crew of the *Dei Gratia*.

The Attorney-General rose obediently at the registrar's demand, allowed the chamber to empty, and then dawdled to his robing room, in expectation of the nightly invitation from Cochrane. He had come to welcome the sessions.

After twenty minutes, he emerged, curious. The building seemed empty and deserted. He found Baumgartner in his office, preparing to leave.

'Early night?' he said casually. It would be ill-fitting to make an open enquiry about the judge.

'Coming to need them,' said the registrar. 'These proceedings are taking longer than I anticipated.'

'I warned you I would extend them as long as I thought it would take to come to the truth of the matter.'

'You did that,' remembered the official. He gathered his papers into his briefcase.

'And I believe we're uncovering a strange state of affairs,' added the Attorney-General.

'There are some strange aspects,' conceded Baumgartner. He seemed to hesitate, waiting for Flood to continue the conversation, then said, 'I am afraid you must excuse me.'

'Of course,' said Flood, 'I'll walk with you to my carriage.'

'The judge wanted to get away early tonight,' offered Baumgartner, falling into step. 'So he won't be very pleased.'

'Pleased?' queried Flood.

'By the request from Mr Pisani for an application in chambers.'

'No,' agreed Flood immediately, perfectly concealing any reaction. 'I'm sure he won't.'

Thirty minutes later he was sitting, as was his custom before dinner, upon the balcony of his home overlooking the Spanish mainland. Tonight he was unaware of the view, immersed in thought. What application was Pisani making in the privacy of the judge's rooms? And on a day when, for the first time, the objections to cross-examination had remained strangely muted? There could only be one logical explanation, decided the Attorney-General. The man had become unhappy with his clients' case. And was attempting to preserve his integrity by communicating that unhappiness to the man heading the enquiry. His reflections were interrupted by the arrival of a messenger, carrying the transcripts of the day's hearing. Flood sat gazing down at them, musing. If his surmise was correct, it made it even more important to send his account as quickly as possible to London, to show the authorities, just how astute he had been from the very beginning in recognising the falsehood. He took up the evidence, hurrying to the study in which, so very recently, he had been confronted by Dr Patron's stupidity. Now that seemed almost immaterial.

He had been working for almost an hour when there was movement at the door and he looked up at the housekeeper, who announced that dinner was ready.

'I'm not eating tonight. Too busy,' he said hurriedly.

'A tray?' enquired the woman.

'Nothing,' said the Attorney-General, curtly. He had more important things to attend to than food. Far more important.

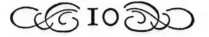

10

There had been a brief lull, insufficient even to launch the boat to examine the splintering to the hull, and then one of the worst gales they had experienced set in, casting the ship about in such seas that it had been almost impossible to steer. The whole crew had had to turn to, so that it had been impractical to hold their customary Sunday prayer gathering, which Briggs had regretted. He had spared himself for a few moments from the deck just before Sarah had retired and they had prayed together, Briggs not thinking his wife over-dramatic for choosing as their hymn 'For Those in Peril on the Sea'. He knew how concerned she was about the baby.

'If anything happened, you'd save Sophia, wouldn't you?'

He stared at her:

'Happened?'

'You know what I mean.'

'Nothing is going to happen. It's just a bad voyage, that's all.'

The strange conversation had surprised him because he had believed her anxiety was over, now that Sophia had got her sea legs. The sickness had stopped and for the past two days she had been able to extend her diet to eggs and boiled fish. The weather had confined her to the cabin, but she was still weak and had not so far complained. Briggs was sure her health as well as her spirits would improve once they reached the warmth and shelter of the Mediterranean.

At first light, Sarah's hymn proved more apposite than Briggs had imagined. Goodschall, who was standing watch, saw the other ship first, more than a mile to the lee and carrying far too much sail for the weather.

Richardson had summoned the captain, to approve the change

of course, and for over an hour they had tacked to get nearer, to give what assistance they could. The seas were still high, so that their view of the ship was sporadic and they were still some way off when they lost sight of the sail.

Briggs decided it was too dangerous to send a look-out even part-way up the pitching mast and so they had continued on the course of the last sighting. Unasked, William Head brought from the galley everything disposable and stayed at the stern, casting it adrift at intervals so that they had a rough marker of their passage; when, by ten o'clock, Briggs decided they had crossed the point at which they had last seen the vessel, he was able to turn and retrace his route.

It was noon when they spotted what remained and then it was hardly enough to decide what sort of vessel she had been. The torn sail lay spread over the water and a shattered spar stuck up, held oddly in position by something unseen beneath the water.

Because it was impossible to know how much remained hidden underneath the sail, and aware of the potential danger to his own hull, Briggs hove-to some way off, putting out a sea anchor despite the swell. Goodschall volunteered to go up the mast to look for survivors. The Lorensen brothers lashed him into a safety line and remained at the foot of the mast, holding the rope in case he lost his footing.

After thirty minutes, the young German gestured that there was nothing he could see and Briggs brought him down. Both Richardson and Briggs had been sweeping the sea through glasses and now they concentrated upon the wreckage.

'Could be part of a gaff,' said Richardson, looking at the spar jutting from the water.

'Might have been a brig, like us.'

'Why was she carrying so much sail?' wondered Gilling, who had joined them at the rail. 'Not as if the storm were sudden, after all.'

'Could have been illness aboard, with not enough hands to work her,' said Richardson.

'Then whoever remained should have short-sailed her,' pointed out Briggs. He turned, seeing Sarah and recognising immediately her need for comfort. He moved away from the mates, putting his arm around her shoulders. It was a gesture his father would have criticised, in front of the crew.

'Poor souls,' she said, quietly.

'Goodschall has looked for a long time. There's no sight of anyone,' said Briggs.

'I know,' said Sarah. She shivered. 'How can it happen, as quickly as that? Not three hours ago it was a ship, with people aboard. We could see it ... '

She threw her arm out.

' ... now that's all there is left.'

'Sometimes it's very quick,' said Briggs.

'But so little ... just a sail and piece of wood.' Fear shuddered through her again. 'I must pray for them,' she said.

'We all must,' said Briggs. 'Go back to the cabin.'

'No,' refused the woman, knowing that her husband was concerned that they might still come upon some bodies. 'Sophia is content enough.'

'Shall we put the boat out?' asked Richardson.

Briggs shook his head. 'Little point,' he said. 'And in this sea it would be far too easy for that spar to be driven through the hull. We'll circle.'

The wind was still strong, so that it was a difficult manoeuvre. The stuck-up spar seemed to follow them around, rocking back and forth with the waves, like a gesturing finger. Occasionally the water broke over other debris clinging to the sail, proof that Briggs's caution was well founded. Satisfied that no one was caught up or clinging to the wreckage they could see, Briggs continued to work the *Mary Celeste* in gradually widening circles.

There was no further trace of what, only a few hours before, had been a vessel as big as theirs.

After another hour, Briggs said to Richardson: 'There's nothing. Resume course.'

Richardson gave the order to Martens, at the helm, then came back to the captain.

'It's frightening,' he said. The sail was some way off now, the spar still beckoning.

'Yes,' said Briggs. 'There'll be a lot of that in the Atlantic this winter, after the weather we've been meeting.'

'Hope I'm not the one to come upon it,' said the first mate.

The effect of the disaster was immediate. Always a quiet ship, the *Mary Celeste* became quieter. Beyond orders from Briggs, there was virtually no talk. Men who knew the power of the sea and who therefore had no reason to be embarrassed by their feelings, they still moved about with eyes lowered against contact, each as if his fear were different from the other man's, a weakness to be hidden.

They only looked up to stare out at the heaving water, aware that they were many cables distant from where the unknown ship had foundered, but wondering if the same waves which had smashed a ship to oblivion could, by the same capriciousness, cast its crew into their path, to safety.

They secured lashings extra-tightly and checked the bindings of the furled sails, and the Lorensen brothers found a reason to examine the ship's boat, ensuring that it could be easily slipped from its fenders and that the water canisters were easily to hand.

It was not until the evening, and then perhaps because the weather began to improve, that the feeling began to lift from the vessel. Briggs stood aft with Richardson, behind the helmsman, looking out at the slackening water.

'Wonder if it will last this time?' he said.

'Pray to God it does,' said the first mate. 'The earlier improvements have been short enough lived.'

'How's the splintering?'

'As far as I can see from the decking, there's been some wood shorn off, but its finished now. There's still no leakage.'

A wave swept the deck, fountaining up over the hatch-covers.

'There's no doubt about the seepage from the barrels,' added Richardson.

'Any way of knowing how much?'

'Not until we can lift the covers. And even then, it wouldn't be practical to examine every barrel.'

Reminded by Martens's presence at the wheel, Briggs said, 'I'm gladdened that so many are going to stay with the ship.'

Richardson nodded. 'I wish every crew were as good,' he said. 'The younger of the Lorensen brothers is after making his fortune before he marries.'

'Whatever the reason for their staying, it's good news for us.'

'And there won't be the worry over the return cargo that there is with this,' said Richardson.

'After this crossing, I wouldn't object to a little time in port,' said Briggs. 'For Sophia's sake, particularly.'

'May I show you something?' said Richardson.

'Of course.'

'In my cabin.'

Briggs followed the first mate to his quarters, smiling as he approached at the sound of Sarah's melodeon. Her feelings were improving along with everyone else's.

'I didn't know what plans you had made,' said Richardson, when they got into his living quarters. 'But it's likely that we'll all be aboard for Christmas. I'm carving this for the baby.'

Although still roughly shaped, it was clearly a replica of the *Mary Celeste*. The detail around the bowsprit was perfect.

'A souvenir of her first voyage,' said the chief mate. The pride was very evident.

'It's a fine gesture, Mr Richardson,' said Briggs. 'I'm grateful. Mrs Briggs will be, too. I can foresee battles between the baby and Arthur when we get home.'

'There's still a month before Christmas,' said Richardson. 'There will be time to do one for him, too.'

'It'll not only be a reminder for the child,' said Briggs, 'it will be a memory for me, my first voyage as owner-captain.'

Sarah stopped playing as Briggs entered his quarters. He stopped, taking Sophia into his arms but holding her out, so that her face was opposite his.

'She's still pale,' he said.

'The sun will soon cure that.'

'No more sickness?'

'Two eggs for supper. And some bread.'

'In New York, she was eating hash and meat,' he remembered.

'Give her time,' said Sarah.

Briggs drew the baby close to him.

'The first mate is carving her a Yuletide present,' he said.

'It would have been nice to be home before Christmas,' said Sarah.

Briggs sat on the couch, still holding the child. She began groping into an accustomed pocket, seeking his silver watch. He pulled it out and held it to her ear. She smiled at the ticking, moving her head in time to the sound.

'I'll not enjoy the festival without Arthur,' continued the woman. 'He's at an age when these things are important.'

'Richardson is making a gift for him, too.'

'I can't clear my mind of what happened today,' said Sarah.

'She was badly rigged,' said Briggs, trying to reassure her. 'It could never have happened with the sort of crew we've got.'

'Do you know what I've been thinking?'

'What?'

Tired of the watch, Sophia clambered from her father's lap and went to where she had left a rag doll, beside the desk. 'I wonder if there were any children aboard, like Sophia.'

'You mustn't dwell upon it,' said Briggs gently. 'It might have been an old ship ... unseaworthy. There's more danger from a horse-drawn buggy in Marion's Main Street than there is crossing the Atlantic in the *Mary Celeste*.'

She smiled thinly, trying to respond to his lightness.

'I know we're secure enough,' she said. 'I thought that, too, looking down at that torn sail today. Poor people, whoever they were.'

'There must have been some good reason for them ignoring the rigging like that.'

'How horrible,' said the woman. 'Imagine being too sick to do anything, feeling your ship being thrown about and knowing disaster was about to happen.'

Although it was unlikely that everyone could have perished in the same way, there was always the possibility that the crew of the unknown vessel had been swept overboard before they had even sighted her. Briggs decided not to mention the thought to his wife. It wasn't a discussion he wanted to prolong.

'There'll be sight of land soon,' he said. 'The Azores.'

'Will we make port there?'

Briggs shook his head.

'We've lost enough time as it is,' he said. 'I'll continue for Gibraltar.'

'I wonder if the *Dei Gratia* will be there,' said Sarah.

Briggs remembered his wife's reservations about Captain Morehouse.

'You'll not forget my invitation?' he said.

She looked up from her sewing, faintly annoyed at the reminder.

'I've promised you he'll be welcome at our table,' she said.

In the galley, where the crew had taken their meal, speculation about the identity and cause of the wreck had continued unabated for two hours.

Volkert Lorensen thrust his cup aside during a break in the conversation and said, 'It might have seemed a fair reservation in New York, but after the sort of crossing we're enduring, I'd welcome something a little stronger than coffee.'

Goodschall waved his hand in the direction of the bulkhead. 'There's drink enough in the holds,' he said. 'Gallons of it.'

'Commercial alcohol!' laughed Richardson. 'Have you smelt it?'

'Impossible not to,' complained Gilling.

'Believe me,' said the first mate, 'it tastes worse than it smells. Commercial alcohol is undrinkable.'

11

Frederick Flood liked bullfights.

He did not see them, as they were frequently dismissed by faint-hearted tourists, as gory, orgiastic spectacles. Or even as the simplistic illustrations of courage, man against primitive beast, of which the Spanish *aficionados* spoke. He liked to sit in an arena and imagine the emotions of the matador, conjuring in his own mind the fear the man would know in the early moments of confrontation, when one mistake could mean death, and then the other feeling, the sensation of which he was even more convinced, the almost sensuous euphoria that must come at the fighter's realisation that he was going to win. It must be very similar to the feeling he knew now, thought the Attorney-General, as he watched the swearing-in of his first witness.

Even the fact that Sir James had not that morning summoned him, as the Attorney-General had anticipated, to tell him of the previous night's discussions in chambers, failed to affect his humour. He was quite convinced that his view of Pisani's integrity was correct and that some indication would come during the course of the day's hearing.

From his bench, Cochrane looked invitingly at Flood, who rose to begin his examination. John Austin, the colony's surveyor of shipping, regarded him expectantly. It took only moments to establish the man's qualifications as an expert witness.

'Did you, on December 23 of last year, accompany myself and Mr Vecchio, the marshal of this court, aboard a half-brig known as the *Mary Celeste*?' opened Flood. The time for nuance was over. Now it was to be the straight presentation of unarguable facts.

'Yes,' said Austin.

'For what purpose?'

'To carry out as thorough an examination as was practicable and from that examination conclude the reason for the ship's supposed abandonment.'

'Was such an examination possible?'

'Yes.'

'How long were you so occupied?'

'Five hours.'

'What was the first thing you found?'

'On approaching the vessel I discovered damage to the bow between two and three feet above the waterline on the port side. A long, narrow strip at the edge of one of her outer planks under the cathead was cut away to a depth of about three-eighths of an inch and about one inch and a quarter wide for a length of six to seven feet.'

'Could it have been caused by the adverse weather conditions we are all aware have recently been affecting the Atlantic?' broke in Flood, anxious that the point should be established.

'In my opinion, no,' asserted Austin. 'It was recently sustained and was apparently done by a sharp cutting instrument continuously applied through the whole length of the injury. On the starboard bow a little farther from the stem I discovered a precisely similar injury, but perhaps an eighth or a tenth of an inch wider.'

'Could this have been caused by the weather?' repeated the Attorney-General.

'No,' said Austin. 'In my opinion, it had been caused at the same time as the damage to the starboard side. And by the same sharp cutting instrument.'

'There has been much conjecture during the course of this enquiry,' said Flood. 'The most frequent is that some bizarre weather condition caused the inexplicable abandonment of the *Mary Celeste* by its crew. Would you assist the court by giving your judgment upon such a possibility?'

Austin turned to the judge, knowing the importance the Attorney-General placed upon the question and wanting Cochrane to misunderstand nothing:

'I do not think that the *Mary Celeste* ever encountered weather severe enough for her crew to have considered abandoning her in favour of a ship's boat.'

Flood was aware of the stir at the lawyers' bench and then of the movement in the court, where the earlier witnesses were sitting. Pisani's unhappiness would be increasing with every moment that passed.

'You have no doubt about that?' Flood pressed.

'Absolutely none.'

'That view is obviously supported by evidence?'

'Of course,' said Austin.

'Then taking as much time as you feel necessary, Mr Austin, perhaps you could provide that evidence.'

There was more movement from where the lawyers sat as they prepared to take notes.

'The *Mary Celeste* has no bulwarks, but a top-gallant rail supported by stanchions,' began the surveyor. 'The whole of this rail, apart from one section, was uninjured. Nor was a single stanchion misplaced. Upon the deck were water barrels, in their proper places and secured. Had the vessel ever been thrown on her beam ends or encountered a very serious gale, the barrels would have gone adrift, carrying away some of the top-gallant stanchions.'

'That is your only evidence?'

'By no means. There is a for'ard deckhouse, made of thick planking and painted white, the seam between it and the deck being filled with pitch. A very violent sea would have swept the deckhouse away. A sea of less than very great violence would have cracked the panelling or the pitch. It had not suffered the slightest injury; there was not even cracking in the paint. I examined the windows and shutters of this deckhouse. None was damaged in the slightest degree, as they would have been had bad weather been encountered.'

'What else?'

'On the starboard side of the main cabin was the chief mate's quarters. On a little bracket in this cabin I found a small phial of oil for a sewing machine, in an upright, perpendicular position, a reel of cotton and a thimble. Such light articles would have been cast down in any serious gale. In a lower drawer beneath the bedspace was a quantity of glass and some loose pieces of iron, stored together. I would have expected this iron to shatter the glass, had the *Mary Celeste* been thrown about. The glass was intact. Throughout the vessel, there were windows the glass of which was not of the reinforced, porthole type. Unless covered or shuttered in bad weather – and none of it was covered when I boarded the vessel – then this glass would have been stove in by heavy seas.'

'Would you help the court about what you found upon descending through the lazarette hatch?'

'As the court knows, this is the storage area of the vessel,' responded Austin. 'I located here several barrels of assorted stores and also a barrel of Stockholm tar, the head of which had been removed. Neither the provisions nor the tar had been upset by weather, as would have undoubtedly happened if it had been bad.'

'Will you now talk about your findings in the master's cabin?'

During his evidence, Austin had turned slightly away from Cochrane, towards the court. He went back now, knowing it was another important piece of evidence.

'There was a sword there, of a somewhat ornate design –' began Austin.

'This sword?' queried Flood, offering the exhibit.

The marshal carried it to Austin, who nodded.

'Yes,' he said. 'This was the weapon. I examined it minutely. I did not consider it affected by the water which had wetted, although not to an appreciable degree, other sections of the vessel. Upon withdrawing the blade from its scabbard, I saw upon the blade marks which I believed to be blood. Attempts had been made to wipe them away –'

'A moment, Mr Austin,' interrupted the Attorney-General. 'Let us establish a fact here without question of challenge. Although not substantial, is it your view that there were areas of the ship which had been wetted by the sea and this cabin was one of them, apparently having had an open fanlight when the salvage crew boarded?'

'That was my information.'

'That being so, do you consider that the marks upon this sword could have been in any way those of rust, caused by that wetting?'

'As I have already said, no, I do not.'

'You have no doubt whatsoever that the stains were blood?'

'None. There had been some attempts to wipe the blade, but it was still clearly blood.'

The Attorney-General paused, glancing to his right. All three lawyers sat hunched over their pads, writing hurriedly.

'Did you discover any wine, beer or spirits aboard?'

'No, sir, none.'

'You have told us that, in your opinion, no weather conditions could have caused the abandonment of the *Mary Celeste*. During the five hours you spent conducting your minute, expert examination did you come upon any other logical explanation of why Captain Briggs should have taken his wife, baby and crew off in the ship's boat?'

'Absolutely none. I studied every part of the ship to which I had access in an effort to discover whether there had been any explosion or whether there had been any fires or any accident calculated to create an alarm of an explosion or fire. I did not discover the slightest trace of such a thing.'

'The vessel was sound and not shipping water to any appreciable extent?'

'Absolutely sound.'

'You had a diver, Mr Ricardo Portunato, conduct an external examination of the hull?'

'I did.'

'What were his findings?'

'The hull was intact, in excellent condition and with no visible signs of damage other than the two cut marks about which I have already spoken.'

'What conclusions do you, an expert, draw from all this, Mr Austin?'

'From my examination of the *Mary Celeste*, I did not discover any evidence indicating weather conditions or any other logical explanation for the disappearance of the crew.'

'Continuing that assessment to its logical end, can there only be a sinister conclusion as to the fate of Captain Briggs, his wife, their child, and perhaps some of the crew?'

'I fear so,' said Austin.

The Attorney-General sat down, flushed with contentment. Returning to his reflections at the beginning of the day, he decided that had he been performing in the bullring and not in a court, he would surely have been awarded not just the ears, but the tail as well.

He relaxed in his seat, watching first Pisani and then Cornwell attempt to obtain from the surveyor some qualification of the dogmatic evidence he had given. Austin remained absolutely unshakeable, repeating again and again that there had been no evidence aboard the ship to support the theory that the vessel had been beset by gales.

For a lawyer who could no longer have any belief in his brief, Pisani was questioning with remarkable tenacity. Flood regarded the man admiringly. Pisani *did* have integrity. But it was proving to little avail. The more Pisani tried, the worse he made it sound for the crew of the *Dei Gratia*.

The Attorney-General decided he would invoke the request with which he had ended each day's examination and have Oliver Deveau recalled. John Austin's evidence would make a damaging contrast to that of the first mate, and Flood judged Deveau more likely to collapse under positive challenge than either Morehouse or Winchester. The Attorney-General felt he could afford to wait, savouring their eventual capitulation to truth at some later time.

He looked casually around, unable to locate Deveau. Obviously the man had absented himself for a few moments; Flood had been passingly aware of how accustomed these men had become to court proceedings, leaving and entering during the course of the hearing, no longer sniggering like nervous schoolboys, as they had that first day. It was true, of course, that even the most obtuse must recognise which way the hearing was going and realise that there was little cause for laughter any more.

It was a further hour before Pisani conceded defeat, sitting down and leaving the surveyor with every statement absolutely intact.

Flood was on his feet as soon as the surveyor had been released.

'I seek the recall of Oliver Deveau,' he announced.

The response came not from the court registrar, as he had anticipated, but from Pisani.

'I regret that will not be possible,' said the crew lawyer, standing.

Cochrane looked up enquiringly.

'Why not?' he demanded.

'You will recall, sir, that I made application to you last night in chambers for the formal release from custody of the *Dei Gratia*,' reminded the lawyer.

'Yes,' agreed Cochrane doubtfully.

Bird-like, Flood sat with his head to one side, the attitude of a sparrow which has had the worm snatched from it by a crow. Outrage engulfed him, fleeting anger at his misconception of the purpose of Pisani's private interview and then at the judge's stupidity in releasing the salvage vessel. With difficulty, he controlled any outward sign of emotion, remembering from Cochrane's clashes with the other lawyers how quick the man was to respond to criticism.

'It was thought best that Captain Morehouse, as the senior officer, should remain here to give continuing assistance to the court, and that Deveau should take the *Dei Gratia* on to Genoa to unload,' said Pisani, uncomfortably aware of the judge's impending reaction.

'What!' demanded Cochrane. 'Thought better by whom?'

'Myself, Captain Morehouse … and we sought the advice of Captain Winchester,' stumbled the lawyer.

'Did I not make it clear that the release was subject to its creating no inconvenience whatsoever to this enquiry?'

'Yes, My Lord, you did,' conceded Pisani.

What a cabal, thought Flood. They had reached the same conclusion as he, that Deveau might be the first to collapse. And tried to shift him away to where he could cause least harm.

'But Captain Morehouse never boarded the *Mary Celeste*,' protested the judge, his indignation matching that which Flood had felt minutes before. 'What possible purpose could there be in his staying in preference to a witness as vital as the man who commanded the vessel throughout its days of salvage?'

Cochrane was stressing his annoyance, anxious to recover from what he must now recognise to be a mistake, decided the Attorney-General. First the analyst. Now the judge. Thank God he was sending his reports to London where they could be assessed without interference from fools.

'It would seem that a miscalculation has been made,' admitted Pisani.

'Indeed there has, sir,' said Cochrane. 'I am adjourning this hearing today, to enable you and Captain Morehouse to communicate with the ship-owners and with the consul in Genoa, ordering Deveau back to the precincts and jurisdiction of this court by the fastest means at his disposal. And let me make it quite clear to you and everyone else in this chamber, Mr Pisani: I will not have the authority of this court impugned or endangered again, sir! Is that understood?'

'It was never the intention of anyone to impugn your authority,' attempted Pisani humbly.

'Of that, sir, I remain to be convinced,' said Cochrane, jerking to his feet to end the confrontation.

This time the request to visit the chambers came almost as soon as the Attorney-General had disrobed. There was no invitation to sherry as Flood settled himself.

Closer than he had been to the man in court, Flood saw that Cochrane was flushed with anger, a nerve in his eyelid tugging in annoyance and creating the ludicrous impression that the man was winking conspiratorially.

'What do you make of it?' demanded Cochrane immediately. He put his hand up, to cover his flickering eye.

'There can be only one conclusion,' said the Attorney-General. He would be failing in his duty as Admiralty Proctor if he did not include in that night's report to London an account of the mistake that Sir James had made.

'Do you think he'll return?' said the judge.

'It's impossible to say,' suggested Flood. 'You could always pass on the request through London for the British Consul in Genoa to urge some action from the American representatives there.'

Cochrane frowned, aware that the request would confirm his error to the Admiralty.

'I've the assurance from Pisani that everything will be done,' he said awkwardly.

He paused, as if debating whether to continue. Then he said, 'I have decided to call in the police authorities and make available to them a transcript of everything that has been said at this enquiry.'

'I had hoped you would,' said Flood honestly.

'I'm not hopeful, though.'

'Hopeful?'

'Unless there's an admission of conspiracy from someone ... of any criminality, in fact, then I don't think there's sufficient evidence for a criminal arrest.'

Winchester's anger was greater because of his realisation that he had made an error and that it would add to the suspicion already created.

'I didn't think of bail-bond money,' he protested.

'Unless a surety is lodged with the court against any subsequent claim, you'll not get the return of the *Mary Celeste*,' predicted Cornwell.

'I should have been advised,' said the owner.

'I didn't think a reminder would be necessary,' said Cornwell defensively. 'Isn't there anyone who will honour a note from you?'

Winchester considered the question. There was a broker whom he had known in Cadiz. But the man had died the previous year.

'Not that I can ... ' he began, then stopped. The day he had left New York for Gibraltar, the *Daisy Boynton* had lifted anchor with a cargo also for Cadiz. Captain Henry Appleby had been a schoolfriend of his daughter; they had even discussed a possible social meeting during their chance encounter at the shipping commission office.

'Maybe,' he corrected.

'I think you should consider arranging it,' said Cornwell. 'I think we should take every care to avoid antagonising the court further.'

'The judge is not convinced that sending Deveau to Genoa was a genuine misunderstanding,' warned the American Consul. He had not anticipated that the affair would become as difficult as it had. Or as protracted. Washington's interest surprised him.

'The damned man is convinced of only one thing, like the Attorney-General,' said Winchester. 'I tell you, Mr Sprague, I'm worried. Very worried indeed.'

As always in their after-court discussions, the New York shipowner roamed the room, too indignant to sit.

'Did you know that Flood and Cochrane have nightly con-
ferences, after the hearing!' said Cornwell.

'At which the discussions are a good deal less innocent than the
conversations we have here, I'll be bound,' said Morehouse.

Winchester stopped parading, looking intently at Sprague.

'Why don't you complain officially through Washington that
American citizens are being harassed here?' he suggested. 'Get
them to take it up with London.'

'Captain Winchester,' said Pisani warningly, 'can you imagine
how that would appear, while a court was still in session considering a claim for salvage? There's enough suspicion being cast
about as it is, without our contributing to it by raising with your
government something that could be construed as our having
something to hide.'

'I'm damned if I'll sit here and do nothing,' said Winchester.
'This is more like an inquisition of the Middle Ages.'

Pisani appeared embarrassed, looking up at the bespectacled
ship-owner:

'As I left the court tonight the Attorney-General's clerk advised
me that, in Deveau's absence, Flood intended to recall you tomorrow morning.'

'They're out to get me, any way they can,' accepted Winchester
softly.

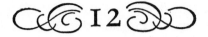

12

The importance of recognising crew behaviour had been one of the earliest lessons he had received from his father and Briggs accepted realistically that with any other crew, upon a voyage such as they had endured since leaving New York, trouble would have erupted far sooner. And probably far more violently. But when it came, it still surprised him and initially his annoyance was not so much by what Boz Lorensen and Gottlieb Goodschall had done but at his unpreparedness for it. No matter how good a crew they had proved to be, he should still have been aware of the constant strain imposed by the squalls and gales, which meant that they had only been able to rest for the minimum of time and then perhaps had not slept away the fatigue from the unremitting work throughout their periods of watch. And now the gales were lessening, albeit very slightly, the weather had become thundery, covering everything with a sultry, oppressive heat. He should have been aware of the explosive potential, just as he should have known that the incident of the sinking ship, reminding them all how vulnerable they were even in a vessel as sound as the *Mary Celeste*, would provide the fuse.

He had been taking his last turn on deck, standing very near Volkert Lorensen at the conn, when the argument had broken out in the fo'c'sle, so he had been able to hear it. The first mate had heard it, too, even though his quarters were farther away, and Richardson reached the dispute first.

By the time Briggs had entered the crews' quarters, the younger Lorensen and Goodschall had been pulled apart and Richardson had positioned himself between them. The two seamen stood panting, glowering at each other. A bruise was already forming beneath Goodschall's right eye but apart from that there appeared to be no injury to either man. In the scuffle, some of the playing cards that Briggs had banned before the voyage commenced had spilled over on to the floor.

As soon as he saw the captain enter, Boz Lorensen thrust his hand towards the other German and said, 'My money. He stole some of my money.'

'I did not,' said Goodschall, denying the accusation immediately.

'My cabin.' Briggs stopped them, refusing an impromptu hearing. 'Nine tomorrow.'

Sarah was already preparing to retire, her long hair streamed over her shoulder as she brushed it, when he returned to the cabin. She listened without interruption as he told her of the fight, hair brush cupped in her lap.

'Appears a small thing,' she said, when he had finished.

'Not if there's been cheating or theft,' contradicted Briggs. 'I should have anticipated the possibility of trouble.'

'The weather has affected us all,' said the woman. 'First the gales, now this heat. It's dulling us.'

'A captain can't afford to be dulled,' he said. He hesitated, then decided against telling her that no doubt carelessness had caused the tragedy upon which they had come the previous day.

'To magnify it too much would be as great an error, don't you think?' she asked sensibly.

'You're right,' he agreed. He wouldn't be caught unawares again, he determined.

The contrition of both men was obvious immediately they entered his cabin the following morning. The bruise had worsened on Goodschall's face, blackening his cheek and half-closing his eye. Both stood with caps held before them, staring down.

The circumstances of the dispute, outlined by the first mate, were as simple as the argument itself. The playing cards had been brought aboard by Lorensen, who insisted that he had had no intention of disobeying the captain's orders against engaging in games of chance. Goodschall admitted complaining of boredom after such an arduous crossing, and at first they had only engaged in tricks, starting a game only when the amusement had begun to wane.

Goodschall had been the loser and when Lorensen had returned from a visit to the heads he had discovered some money missing.

'Did you take it, to make up for what you had lost?' demanded Briggs. On a ship as small as his, with the men having to occupy confined quarters, stealing was a serious crime.

Before Goodschall could reply, Lorensen blurted out, 'I found it.'

'Found it?' said Briggs.

'I'd put some in my pocket. I forgot about it.'

Briggs sighed. Now that there was no question of dishonesty, the matter assumed far less importance. But there was still the disobedience of a captain's order to be considered.

'I expressly forbade wagering for precisely the reason that you two are standing before me now,' he said. 'The ship is too small and, as it's transpired, the voyage too difficult for bad feeling to be allowed over a gambling dispute. Wasn't that made clear enough?'

'We didn't set out to play,' repeated Lorensen. 'It just … sort of developed.'

This man was guiltier than Goodschall, decided Briggs. He remembered Richardson's remark about Lorensen's keenness to acquire money. He would resent paying the fine that Briggs intended to levy. He wondered if the resentment would linger in the fo'c'sle. The Lorensen brothers and Arien Martens all came from the same small island, he remembered. It was easy to imagine the ostracism that could arise in the crews' quarters.

'It won't occur again,' promised Goodschall.

'Of that I'll make quite sure,' said Briggs. 'I'm confiscating the cards.'

Such action might be regarded as petty, he knew. But Briggs decided it would be better for any bad feelings to be transferred to him than confined to the crew area.

He looked at the younger Lorensen. 'I consider you more culpable,' he said, 'because you knowingly ignored an order and brought the cards on board. I'll therefore fine you five dollars.'

He turned to Goodschall:

'And you knowingly entered into the game, well aware it was forbidden. Your penalty will be three dollars.'

For men earning thirty dollars a month, it was severe enough for them to appreciate that he regarded what they had done as serious but not excessive enough to be considered unjust. He would log it, he decided, but not list it in their seamen's books or in any report at the end of the voyage.

Richardson remained after the two men had been dismissed.

'Weather is improving again,' he said. He made a movement to clear his sweat-wet shirt from his back. 'Good rainstorm might flatten the sea even more. And get rid of this confounded heat.'

'I'd like to be able to ventilate today,' said Briggs.

'So would I,' said Richardson. 'The smell has become so bad that the men are complaining in the fo'c'sle. The cook says it's even giving his food a taint.'

'Seepage must be quite heavy.'

'And this heat will make things worse.'

'Perhaps we should risk shipping some water down there anyway. The pumps are more than adequate.'

Richardson moved his head doubtfully.

'I wonder if that ship we came upon yesterday had any hatches off,' he said. 'Must have been something very odd to take her down as quickly as that.'

It would be a long time before any of them forgot that tragedy, Briggs knew.

'It's a question of balancing the risk,' said Briggs. 'We've sailed too long battened down.'

'There's still a high sea running. We're shipping water almost all the time.'

'I think it might be dangerous to wait longer,' said Briggs.

When he emerged on deck, Briggs saw that Sarah considered the child sufficiently recovered to be allowed the run of her safety line. His wife had attached her own line immediately after Sophia's and was guiding the child along the tilted deck with an arm around her shoulders. Sophia was laughing aloud, amused at a new game. Even the occasional spray did not seem to distress her.

Martens was at the helm, smiling that at last mother and daughter were getting some use from the harnesses he had made.

'Is that line strong enough to support them both?' asked Briggs. The ropes looked very thin, he thought.

'More than sufficient,' the German assured him. 'I had someone spell me at the wheel when they came out and attached them myself.'

Farther along the deck, Briggs saw that Boz Lorensen and Goodschall had been assigned to work together. It showed foresight on Richardson's part; it was difficult for shipmates to nurture grievances if they shipped side by side. The men were coiling the peak halyard and as he watched Goodschall said something to the [other German and Lorensen grinned as he made his reply.

Briggs turned out to port. Somewhere hidden behind those lowering, thunderous clouds was the Azores archipelago. Even if they maintained the two to three knots they were running now, it would take until the next day before they were near enough to take a sighting from the most easterly island. He hoped it would not be too early in the morning; Sophia would be excited at her first landfall after almost three weeks.

Richardson emerged from the deckhouse and Briggs beckoned him, nodding towards the two Germans whom he had so recently censured.

'That was a wise course, Mr Richardson.'

'Thank you, sir,' said the mate.

'Looks black,' said Briggs, indicating the direction of the unseen islands.

'Just checked the barometer,' said Richardson.

'What's the reading?'

Before the man could reply, a wave larger than the others that morning slid encroachingly over the deck, sweeping the baby's feet from beneath her. She would have fallen had not Sarah been immediately behind to scoop her up. Goodschall moved immediately from the halyard coiling, supporting mother and baby back along the line to where they were nearest to the deck-house and then walking with them to the companion-way. The child was crying, holding her legs bunched beneath her chin to avoid being soaked again.

'It's dropping,' said Richardson miserably.

'So we're in for more storms?'

'Within an hour or so,' said the first mate. 'Isn't there ever going to be a respite?'

Briggs did not reply immediately. He had already been caught unawares with the crew and it had irritated him, even though the incident was a trivial one. And not twenty-four hours earlier had seen the far from trivial effect of a captain exercising insufficient care.

At the last reading, he was at latitude 36.56 N. by longitude 27.20 W., which put almost all the Azores group astern. San Miguel was about 100 miles away, Santa Maria a little farther.

'There'll be protection in the lee of the islands,' he said, turning to include the helmsman in the remark. Briggs paused, making the decision. Then he said, 'We'll set course for Santa Maria. I want calm within the next twenty-four hours, so that we can ventilate.'

'Aye,' accepted Richardson, walking with Briggs towards the cabin where the captain would chart the course alteration.

It was a decision of sensible seamanship, thought Briggs, as he hunched over the mid-Atlantic charts. Just as taking the protection of Staten Island, at the very commencement of the voyage, had been good seamanship. It was a simple plot, taking only minutes to complete. There would be an added advantage, he decided, as Richardson went back to the conn. Now they would be close enough to the island for Sophia to get a clear view.

He returned to the charts, making another calculation. The impending weather would keep them back to seven or eight knots. It would still be some time before they made landfall.

He looked in the direction of the adjoining cabin, from which emerged the sounds of Sarah quietening the distressed child.

If they made Santa Maria's protection by breakfast, they could be ventilated by noon. He pulled from his pocket the silver watch with which Sophia was so fond of playing.

Less than twenty-four hours before the guarantee of absolute safety. He frowned at the thought, finding it theatrical. There had not been the slightest indication that the cargo was entering a dangerous state. Just as it was sensible not to become careless or complacent, so it was important not to imagine problems before they arose. Hadn't he told Sarah that morning that he couldn't allow his judgment to become affected by external influences?

Sarah and Sophia entered from the next cabin, the baby quite recovered.

Briggs picked her up, holding her at arm's-length as he normally did.

'A surprise for you,' he declared, to the child.

'What?' asked Sarah, over the baby's shoulder.

'I've changed course, to get some protection from the islands. She'll be able to see land some time tomorrow.'

'Is it necessary?' asked the woman.

'Yes,' said Briggs. 'Very necessary.'

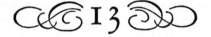

13

Looking at Captain Winchester as he rose to begin his re-examina-
tion, the Attorney-General was again reminded of his bullfighting
analogy. Just as he had earlier felt the euphoria of knowing he
was sure to win, so there was about the New York owner that
ambience of defeat that rises from the bull as the matador positions
himself for the kill, an attitude of defiance that fails to conceal the
beast's awareness that it is confronting a superior opponent.

Flood decided the changed circumstances demanded a different
approach from that upon which he had originally determined for
this third session.

'Your advice was sought before Oliver Deveau was despatched
to Genoa, while Captain Morehouse remained here?' he said.

'It is the custom at sea for the superior officer to be held
responsible for any action or statement of those whom he
commands,' said Winchester. He had removed his pince-nez and
stood leaning slightly forward in the witness box, as if he had
difficulty in focusing upon his interrogator.

Very much like the corrida, thought Flood. Bulls were short-
sighted.

'Just as it is the custom in a court of law for those responsible
for malfeasance to be held guilty of their actions,' said the
Attorney-General. 'But I'm sure the court is grateful for your
definition.'

'I was unaware,' fought back Winchester, 'that this was a court
considering a crime. I believed it to be civil proceedings, adjudg-
ing a civil claim.'

Often, at the very point of death, the bull put up the most
spirited defence, reflected Flood.

'Indeed it is,' he agreed. 'But a legally constituted tribunal would be failing in its function if it failed to respond to the evidence before it.'

'Just as this hearing would be failing in its function if it failed to respond to the evidence before it,' concurred Winchester. 'Having sat in this room for so many days, I still wonder what *evidence* has been established.'

'A responsibility of decision resting upon neither of us,' said Flood. 'But on Mr Justice Cochrane.' And that of the Gibraltar constabulary, he thought. It would be interesting to know what an unbiased observer such as the chief of police would conclude from the statements, affidavits and evidence now before him. Flood had no doubt of the decision.

'Let us move on from the polemics of the judiciary and concentrate upon the statements made since you first stood where you stand today,' he continued. 'If my notation is correct, you asserted during your initial evidence that some manifestation of the weather caused the abandonment of the *Mary Celeste* by Captain Briggs and his crew.'

'Captain Briggs bore a high character, that of a courageous officer and good seaman who would not, I think, desert his ship except to save his life,' said Winchester. 'I also knew the mate, Richardson. I had done so for two years. He was an experienced and courageous officer in whom I had great confidence. I believe he had presence of mind. His three previous captains spoke of him as fit to command any ship and I believe he would not leave his ship except for a matter of life or death. From what I have seen of the state and conditions of the vessel, I cannot believe that she was abandoned by her master, officers and crew by stress of weather only. I had plenty of time to examine her thoroughly and feel very certain that she was not abandoned through perils of the sea.'

Winchester had spoken with urgent seriousness, still anxious to help the enquiry, so that he was breathless when he concluded. For several moments the Attorney-General remained absolutely motionless, giving no reaction whatsoever to the statement. From across the courtroom the owner regarded him defiantly.

Flood waited until his clerk handed him the notes before making any response. As he spoke, the hand holding the papers moved in a vaguely enticing fashion, in the way that the matador lures the exhausted animal on to his sword-point with the flickering of the cape.

' ... cannot believe she was abandoned through stress of weather only,' he paraphrased. 'Nor through perils of the sea ... '

Winchester waited suspiciously.

Flood took great care to select another page of notes, moving it in the same fashion as he had the first.

' ... " It must have been something quite frightening and quite unexpected. It's been a stormy season and I can only assume it was some manifestation of weather that we shall never know" ... '

Flood looked up from his clerk's notes.

'Is that familiar to you, Captain Winchester?' he said.

'I said —' attempted the witness, but Flood interrupted him.

'Is that familiar to you, Captain Winchester?'

'I know that's what I said ... '

'Then what has caused you to alter that statement since you first gave evidence at this enquiry?'

'I have not altered it.'

'To my mind, you have qualified it considerably.'

'I said something quite frightening and unexpected,' tried Winchester.

'And accounted for whatever it was by some unknown weather condition,' the Attorney-General reminded him.

'All I meant to convey was that there was something in addition to the weather.'

'And that addition — something so terrifying that it caused such experienced men to leap overboard — I have been attempting to identify for many days past,' said Flood. 'Having tried once to be more helpful, perhaps you can offer this enquiry the further benefit of your considerable experience. What, beyond stress of weather or known perils of the sea, could have caused such a reaction among such men?'

Wearily Captain Winchester shook his head. There was always such a moment, thought Flood, just before the bull slumped, exposing the fatal point of entry between the shoulder blades.

'If you have the transcript of my earlier evidence before you,' said the ship-owner, 'then I believe you will see that I also stated my belief that no one would ever know ... that it would always remain a mystery.'

'And you may recall my response to that,' replied Flood. 'That before the conclusion of this enquiry, the real truth might be found.'

'I remember the remark well enough,' said Winchester. 'I am unaware of your having succeeded.'

'Then let us proceed and perhaps I might,' said Flood. 'What, in addition to weather or perils of the sea, would cause the abandonment?'

'I don't know!' protested Winchester desperately. 'How many times do we have to have the same question to which I can only make the same answer!'

'We will have the question as many times as it takes me to obtain the *proper* answer,' said Flood. He took up another piece of paper.

'Have you arranged for the *Mary Celeste* to load fruit in Messina, for passage back to New York?' he asked unexpectedly. It had been a wise precaution to have the last three months' editions of the *New York Journal of Commerce* shipped from America, from which he had been able to learn of the contract.

'It was a shipment agreed before I even knew of the disaster that had befallen the vessel,' said the owner.

'If you fail to fulfil that contract, do you stand to lose financially?'

'Of course,' said Winchester. 'I am responsible for my company's bond.'

'Can you afford such loss?'

'Of course not.'

'So you are not a rich man ... you are someone who would welcome money, in fact?'

Until the error with Deveau, that was the sort of question that would have brought Cornwell to his feet in protest. Now the lawyer remained at his bench, hunched in apparent concentration over his papers.

'I am not a rich man,' responded Winchester slowly, as if he were anxious that the judge should be aware of what he was saying. 'For my income I depend upon the workings of my ships. But I am not so short of funds that I am driven to the sort of criminality that has been suggested on numerous occasions at this hearing. I am not involved in any nefarious scheme to benefit

148

from the disappearance and subsequent recovery or the *Mary Celeste*, its crew or any salvage award that this court may feel inclined to make.'

'An assurance, like those that preceded it, which I know this court welcomes,' said Flood, smoothly. He picked up the piece of deck railing, holding it above his head.

'You were aboard the *Mary Celeste* before it sailed from New York?'

'On several occasions.'

Flood gestured to the court marshal for the exhibit to be carried to the owner.

'Do you imagine you would have noticed such an injury on the railing, had it occurred there?'

'Yes, I do. Prior to Captain Briggs's buying into my company, we thoroughly examined the vessel together. There was also a purchaser's survey conducted. It said nothing about any such injury.'

'So it occurred during the voyage?'

'Obviously.'

'How?'

'There are a hundred ways that such damage could have been caused.'

'Would you say it was an axe mark?'

'It is certainly a blow from something heavy.'

'What does that suggest to you?'

Winchester sighed. 'That perhaps there was an incident of the sort that can happen on any ship for a dozen different reasons and that somehow the top-gallant rail became marked.'

'A violent incident?'

The owner looked steadily at the Attorney-General.

'That is your belief,' he said. 'Not mine.'

'Then what is your belief, Captain Winchester?'

'I believe that there occurred aboard the *Mary Celeste* something very extreme but which, were we to know, would be quite understandable to experienced mariners. Whatever it was, it was of sufficient severity to cause two excellent seamen like Captain Briggs and first mate Richardson to quit their ship, something neither of them would have done unless in fear of their lives.'

'And what, this enquiry wonders, would that have been?' said Flood.

'I wish to God I knew, so that I could enlighten you and end this inquisition,' blurted Winchester, unable any longer to hold his anger.

Cochrane came up from his notes and the Attorney-General stood smiling at the reaction he had achieved from the witness.

'Perhaps, when he is returned from the place to which he went upon your advice, first mate Deveau can help us further,' said Flood. 'Since your previous evidence, we have come a long way towards changing your opinion. After the benefit of additional examination of Deveau, it could be that we can achieve more progress.'

Winchester stood regarding the Attorney-General balefully, aware that the outburst of annoyance would be misconstrued in the bias of the hearing.

'You heard the evidence about the sword from the expert witness, surveyor Austin?'

'Yes.'

'And his positive evidence that the stains upon the blade were blood?'

'His *belief* that the stains were blood.'

Flood ignored the qualification.

'Already, Captain Winchester, you have offered the hearing a little more than you did during your first period of evidence,' said the Attorney-General. 'Can you, in advance of anything else we might hear, offer us any further assistance on that staining?'

'How can I?' said Winchester tightly.

'Or on why a supposedly abandoned ship came to be on course?'

'No.'

'Almost as if it had been sailing to a rendezvous?'

'No.'

Perhaps he had moved prematurely for the kill, thought Flood. The witness was proving more resistant than he had anticipated.

'What is your intention, once this enquiry is concluded?' he demanded.

'To retrieve my ship, appoint a new captain and then return to New York to continue my business.'

'What captain?'

'The command has been given to Captain George Blatchford, of Wrentham, Massachusetts.'

The reply appeared momentarily to surprise the Attorney-General.

'What about Captain Morehouse?' he said.

'It is my understanding that Captain Morehouse already has a captaincy, that of the *Dei Gratia*.'

He was losing ground, decided Flood.

'Is it beyond possibility that Captain Morehouse might be offered a position within your company?' he persisted.

'Captain Morehouse and I have the briefest of acquaintance-ships,' said the witness. 'As I have already attempted to make clear to this enquiry, no question of any appointment has been discussed between us.'

'Not for anything Captain Morehouse has done for you?' chanced Flood, heavily.

Pisani moved, as if to stand, but Winchester spoke ahead of any intervention.

'Captain Morehouse returned intact a ship of mine which might otherwise have been lost,' he said. 'For that I am grateful. That is the only service that Captain Morehouse has performed from which I might be regarded as having benefited.'

'Was any suggestion made otherwise?' said Flood.

'Sir,' said Winchester, 'throughout the course of this enquiry suggestions have constantly been made in exaggeration of any evidence to support them.'

'As I have had occasion to remark earlier in the proceedings,' said the Attorney-General, 'the assessment of the evidence and the conclusion to be drawn from it is entirely that of the learned judge.'

'And as I have had occasion to remark,' came back Winchester, 'civil findings in a civil court.'

Flood wondered if he could upset this complacement man's composure by the revelation that the case was now being studied by the police department. Reluctantly he decided against it. The disclosure would be premature and he did not want to provide any opportunity for guilty people to escape.

And Winchester had escaped him again, he accepted. But only

temporarily. Despite every setback, Frederick Flood's determination to bring guilty men to justice had not wavered for a moment.

For the first time during their after-court gatherings, Captain Winchester did not dominate the discussion. Instead, he sat quietly listening to Consul Sprague recount the success they had had in contacting Deveau in Genoa and speeding him back. There was every hope that he would be in Gibraltar in time to give evidence the following day.

'Then perhaps this charade can end,' said Pisani. 'There must *be* a limit to what Cochrane will permit the Attorney-General.'

'I'd like to believe so,' said the other lawyer, Cornwell.

'For some days now I've been regretting that I ever saw the confounded ship and decided to salvage her,' said Morehouse. 'I wish I'd just let her drift on, after assuring myself there was no one on board.'

Aware of how bad that would sound to its owner, the *Dei Gratia* captain looked apologetically towards Captain Winchester.

'I didn't really mean that,' he said hurriedly.

'After the treatment we've received here, it's a natural enough reaction,' said Winchester, unoffended. 'I almost wish you'd let her go myself.'

'Flood seems to be aware of the great interest the finding of this vessel has created in America and England,' said Sprague. 'I think he likes the notoriety he's getting.'

Unaware of the Attorney-General's thoughts in the chamber that day, Winchester said, 'Damned man seems to regard his function to be that of bear-baiting.'

He paused, then looked directly at the consul:

'When I get back to New York I intend filing an official complaint to Washington on the conduct of this enquiry,' he said. 'It's monstrous that these people can behave as they are doing without any apparent check.'

Sprague gestured, indicating the helplessness of his position.

'This is a small colony, a thousand miles from England,' he said. 'Strange though it may seem, I know that Flood and Sir James Cochrane are highly regarded in London.'

'It'll be a short-lived reputation, if I have my way,' vowed the owner.

'The very real problem,' said Pisani seriously, 'is that under the current conditions, there's very little likelihood of your doing so.'

'Given any thought to raising the bail-bond?' Cornwell asked the New York owner suddenly.

'A lot,' admitted Winchester. 'I'm in correspondence with a ship's captain in Cadiz with whom I'm acquainted.'

'Let's hope it will work,' said the lawyer.

'I think it will,' said Winchester.

14

There had been little improvement in the weather, even though they were moving closer to the islands from which they hoped to get shelter. The sea had lessened slightly but the wind stayed near gale force and the first watch took down the royal and top-gallant sails at Briggs's orders; the memory of an over-canvassed ship in a storm was perhaps more vivid in his mind than anyone else's.

Because of the squall, they slept fitfully, always conscious of the pitching of the vessel and the need to adjust their bodies to it, without fully waking.

Only occasionally did Sophia stir, whimpering, and once Sarah got up to her, smiling when she realised the child was only dreaming. For several minutes the woman stood gazing down at her younger child, braced against the ship's movement with her hand against the edge of the tiny cot.

She heard a rumble, seemingly very close, and frowned at the prospect of yet another thunderstorm. Sophia had been remarkably good, decided Sarah, only complaining when she had been sick, which any child would have done. Once her stomach had settled, she had recognised almost without protest that she had to remain within the confines of the cabin, with the few toys they had brought. It was fortunate that his schooling had kept Arthur in Massachusetts. It would have been far more difficult occupying an active seven-year-old than it had been entertaining the baby.

She would be glad to get some sun upon Sophia's face. And feed her up, not just on the fresh meat and fish which would be available in Gibraltar and along the Mediterranean ports, but upon the fruit that she remembered from her previous trips heaped in profusion in every market place.

There was another rumble, more muffled than before, but Sarah was only half aware of the sound, an idea forming in her mind. After such a crossing, the child would benefit from a brief vacation ashore. It would be very easy for them to be set down in one of the French ports on the way to Genoa and then be picked up as the *Mary Celeste* returned. If there were any delays with the return cargo, it would be easy enough for them to make their way overland to rejoin the vessel in port. Monte Carlo or Menton would be pleasant. Or maybe San Remo. If the *Mary Celeste* were detained, it would be quite simple to get to Genoa from any of them.

A spell ashore, no matter how brief, would mean Sophia could get the exercise that hadn't been possible on the cramped, storm-battered ship. They would be able to explore inland villages. And paddle and splash in the sea that had been so cruel to them.

Sarah went slowly back to her bunk, pausing to stare down at her sleeping husband, feeling the warmth of affection. She regarded herself as a fortunate woman; Benjamin Briggs was a good man. And a fine, practising Christian, too. She remembered fondly his discomfort at her recognition of his pride in the *Mary Celeste* that day in New York, the expression on her face similar to that minutes before as she had gazed down at the baby. There was every reason for the feeling, yet her husband would always remain modest, she knew.

She was careful climbing back into her sleeping area, not wanting to disturb him. She was sure he would accept her idea of a holiday as a good one. And, as the pursekeeper, she knew they could afford it easily enough. She would mention it at break-fast.

Briggs had been aware of his wife standing over him, just as he had been aware of her getting up from her bunk and going to the child, but had purposely feigned sleep, not wanting the whispered conversation he knew would ensue if she realised he was awake.

His thoughts were entirely upon the ship. Sarah couldn't help him with that and, adept as she was in recognising his feelings, she would discern his anxiety if they talked. And he did not want to frighten her.

Like her, he had heard the thunder apparently very near and

his worry that he might have changed course too late had increased at the prospect of continuing bad weather. Regardless of the conditions at daybreak, he would open the holds, he decided. The barrels were securely enough stowed, even if they shipped heavy seas. And the pumps would be adequate, providing they kept a careful check.

Despite the decision, the fear that he had waited too long kept intruding itself into his mind. He attempted to recall a long-ago conversation with his father about a shipment of commercial alcohol. He was sure the man had told him there were warning signs before the cargo became volatile, but no matter how he concentrated, he could not bring the recollection to mind.

There was the sound of more thunder and Briggs shifted in his sleeping space, irritated at the memory lapse. Perhaps Richardson would know of it; he would have to ask the first mate early in the morning.

He turned his face towards his wife in the darkness, hearing the deepening breathing and happy that she was getting some rest. Half-sleep came to him at last, while a part of his consciousness lingered over the danger of the ship's cargo and the severity of the weather, so that he was almost immediately aware of the change.

On deck the dropping of the wind which was later to result in a becalming was noticed first around dawn. The sky was streaked with yellow and red when they made the island of Santa Maria, on an east-by-south-easterly bearing. First mate Richardson was actually awakened by the lack of motion in the vessel and got on deck around six. Goodschall, at the helm, gestured ahead and Richardson looked towards the island, jutting up blackly from the water. From his knowledge of the charts, he knew the sighting to be Ponta Cabrastente, on the north-western extremity of Santa Maria.

He went back to the conn.

'What's happening to the weather *now*?' he said.

'Wind has been dropping the past hour,' said the young German.

'Like to be a little closer, to get all the protection we can from the island,' said Richardson reflectively. He turned as the Lorensen brothers came on deck, to change the watch.

'Let's raise the main staysail, to get what wind there is to take us nearer ... '

He looked out at the hardly moving sea.

'Another hour and there won't be any wind at all,' he said, staring back at the sails. Already the upper and lower fore-topsails were sagging and the jib was empty.

'What are we making?' he asked Goodschall.

'Little more than three or four knots,' judged the helmsman. 'It's come right down. During the night, we were managing an almost constant eight or nine.'

Once they were near the protection of Santa Maria, it would be a welcome change, thought Richardson. There was still cloud around the island, which was to be expected. But it was breaking up fairly swiftly over the water; near the horizon there was actually more blue sky than cumulus. It gave an odd effect, like a child's drawing.

Briggs was aloft by seven, brought on deck as much by his decision about the holds as by the changed weather conditions.

'At last,' said Richardson gratefully, as the captain joined him.

'Don't think I'll ever be surprised how quickly things can alter at sea,' said Briggs. The weather meant there was no longer any danger. There was almost a physical feeling, like the easing of a weight upon him, at the realisation.

'I raised the main staysail,' said Richardson. 'To get us as near as possible.'

Briggs nodded approval at the rigging.

'Aye,' he said, looking out to sea. There was little more than a swell running and the *Mary Celeste* rose and fell upon it, scarcely making any way.

'Don't think it's going to achieve much,' he said.

'Knew it would improve, at the island. But I didn't expect this,' said Richardson.

'Nor I,' said Briggs. 'Particularly after the thunder during the night. Thought at one time we were sailing right into it.'

'Yes,' agreed Richardson. 'It really seemed to be building up.'

He turned to Goodschall. 'What time did the storm pass?' he asked casually.

'Wind dropped maybe three hours ago,' said the German.

'How far away was the thunderstorm?'

The younger man frowned at the question.

'There was a blow on,' he said. 'But no thunder.'

'I *heard* it,' insisted Richardson.

'It was very loud,' supported Briggs, suddenly concentrating upon what had begun as a half-considered conversation.

'There was *no* thunder,' repeated Goodschall. 'Not at any time.'

For the moment the three men remained unspeaking at the conn. Then Richardson said, 'There's always a rumbling, before an actual explosion. It's something like the gases all coming up to the boil.'

And Briggs remembered at last what his father had said, all those years ago.

As if on cue, like some awesome theatre, it came again, louder now than at any time before, a grumbling, belching sound from beneath them. It seemed to echo through the entire vessel and there was the impression that the timbers actually vibrated, as they would have done had they been struck repeatedly by something heavy.

At their various positions throughout the deck, everyone stopped what they were doing, straightening and then becoming motionless. Instinctively they were looking to where the captain stood, seeking guidance.

The first movement came from the deckhouse. Sarah appeared, clutching Sophia to her.

'What was it?' she demanded. 'What was that peculiar noise?'

'Dear God,' said Richardson, distantly and to no one, 'don't say we're too late.'

Knowing how little time they had, Briggs jerked forward, calling to the transfixed men around him. Probably there would never again be such a test as this of his qualities as a master-mariner, he thought.

And unless he correctly assessed the situation, there wouldn't be the need, anyway. They were only minutes from being blown to oblivion.

15

The Attorney-General decided it had unquestionably been the best day since the enquiry began. He looked around the hushed chamber, contentedly aware of the effect of the expert witnesses whose affidavits he had produced.

Captain Fitzroy, master of H.M.S. *Minotaur*, had been the first; then Captain Adeane, commanding the *Agincourt*; then Captain Dowell, from the *Hercules*; and finally Captain Vansittart, in command of H.M.S. *Sultan*. There had been no challenge from any of the lawyers because the testimony had been virtually unchallengeable. One after the other the Royal Navy officers had asserted their unequivocal belief that the damage to the *Mary Celeste*'s bows had been caused intentionally, during some act of violence. And they had not limited themselves to the hull marks. They had identified the bloodstaining and unanimously agreed that it was an axe mark on the rail.

Flood looked away from the advocates' bench, towards Sir James Cochrane. They had all wanted evidence and now he had produced it; he had little doubt now that the police would recommend proceedings.

There was a stir from behind and he turned to see the first mate of the *Dei Gratia*, Oliver Deveau, fluster into court. The man's lack of composure was immediately obvious. His usually slicked-down hair was in disarray and even his beard was unkempt.

Pisani rose at his client's entry, beckoning him immediately towards the witness area, turning to the judge as he did so.

'My Lord will see,' he said, in formal apology, 'that we have returned from Genoa the witness whom it was desired to recall.'

'An exercise which would have been unnecessary had the

barest minimum of attention been paid to the needs of this court by the majority of participants,' retorted Cochrane, unmollified.

The Attorney-General concealed any satisfaction at the remark. The judge had obviously been impressed by the evidence of the sea captains.

He rose, determined to attack immediately, gesturing as he did so for Baumgartner to hand the witness the evidence of the captains.

'Having waited for so long, I'm sure the court can spare you for a little further time,' said Flood sarcastically. 'I would like you to read the evidence that has been produced in this court by four expert witnesses.'

Deveau took the affidavits, frowning down. He read slowly, head moving along each page, and the very silence in court was to his advantage, decided the Attorney-General. Cochrane was fidgeting in his seat by the time Deveau looked up.

'Well?' demanded Flood peremptorily.

'Sir?'

'Four experts of unchallengeable integrity have attested on oath before this enquiry that the damage they examined was the result of violence.'

'When I first gave evidence I said I had not noticed the marks to the rail ... or any bloodstaining. And I certainly didn't see any hull damage.'

'A point I accept, Mr Deveau,' said Flood. 'Isn't the problem that you *didn't* see what subsequent examination has discovered?'

'I do not understand,' protested the man.

'Isn't the fact that during the time it took you and your salvage crew to reach Gibraltar there was ample time to repair any evidence of violence ... and that unfortunately you overlooked the axe mark and the bloodstaining that has been found?'

The Attorney-General had expected Deveau to be off-balanced by the questioning, following so closely upon the captains' evidence, but the first mate merely shook his head in persistent denial.

'I also said the first time,' he repeated, 'that we found no evidence of violence. Only of a ship having been abandoned for a number of days.'

Flood concealed his annoyance.

'Why did you leave Gibraltar so hurriedly?' he demanded.

Deveau frowned again. 'There was no haste about it,' he said. 'The *Dei Gratia* had to continue to Genoa, to discharge her cargo. Captain Morehouse ordered me to go.'

'Just as he ordered you to board the *Mary Celeste*?' said Flood.

'Yes –'

'And seize her for salvage?'

Flood was hurrying the questioning, hoping to unsettle the man.

'Captain Morehouse was unwilling at first for us to split the crew,' said Deveau.

The answer was not what Flood had expected and he raised his eyes from his note, examining the witness curiously.

'Explain yourself,' he said.

'When I returned from boarding the *Mary Celeste* I proposed we put a salvage crew aboard. Captain Morehouse said his first responsibility was to his own ship, the *Dei Gratia*, and that he was unhappy at the thought of reducing his crew by the number of men necessary to take over the *Mary Celeste*.'

'So what happened?'

'There was a discussion among the crew, who agreed to do extra watches.'

'Why did they so agree?'

'So that we could man the *Mary Celeste*, of course,' said the man, surprised.

'And in expectation of sharing in a salvage award once she was brought to port?' demanded the Attorney-General.

'Yes,' said Deveau.

'Was there a reduced crew on the *Mary Celeste*?'

'Sir?'

'Was there a reduced crew? Or is the fact of the matter that there were still some people aboard when you crossed to her?'

Deveau shook his head, a familiar gesture of bewilderment.

'The *Mary Celeste* was *abandoned*,' he insisted.

'Are you an obedient seaman?' said Flood, returning to his earlier questioning.

'I pride myself upon being so,' responded Deveau immediately.

'So you would obey any command a superior officer gave you?'

'Were it in keeping with the laws of the sea and ensuring the safety or smooth running of any vessel in which I was serving, then, yes, I would,' said Deveau.

It could almost be construed as a prepared answer, decided Flood.

'Did you, on December 5, receive from Captain Morehouse any order that did not comply with those restrictions?'

'Really!' protested Pisani, rising. 'We are off again on the wildest flights of fancy. Can there be any point to this flagrant innuendo?'

Cochrane looked at the protesting lawyer, then to the Attorney-General:

'Mr Flood?'

'I would not be pursuing this or any other line of questioning if I did not consider it germane to the court's enquiry,' said the Attorney-General.

'An assurance which we have received time upon time and of which we still seek proof,' disagreed Pisani.

'It is proof with which I am attempting to furnish this court.'

'Of what?' demanded the *Dei Gratia* attorney, in open challenge.

'I would have thought by now that would have been obvious to everyone,' said Flood.

'The point of much of your questioning, Mr Flood, remains obvious only to yourself,' said Pisani.

The Attorney-General started to retort, but the judge stopped the dispute.

'I feel,' he said, addressing the Attorney-General, 'that this hearing might proceed in a more satisfactory manner if a certain propriety were maintained in the examination.'

Flood knew that Cochrane could not possibly be against him, after the evidence he had been able to produce. He decided that the judge must be satisfied. But *he* wasn't, determined Flood.

'Have you any cause to change your beliefs as to how the *Mary Celeste* came to be abandoned?' he said.

'No, sir,' said Deveau.

'Or of what fate befell the crew?'

'No, sir.'

'Against the opinions of experts you heard before you hurried away or from the affidavits you have today considered, do you have any wish to change your evidence?'

'I have told the court everything I can to help,' said the first mate.

'Was the need to get the *Dei Gratia* to Genoa to unload its cargo of petroleum the only reason you were despatched from Gibraltar?'

Deveau regarded the Attorney-General uncertainly.

'Yes,' he said, the curiosity sounding in his voice. 'What other reason could there have been?'

'It was not perhaps thought wiser by Captain Morehouse or even by Captain Winchester for you to be hopefully beyond the call of this enquiry?'

Pisani started to rise, but Cochrane anticipated the protest.

'Aren't we risking propriety again, Mr Flood?' he cautioned.

'Only in pursuit of the truth,' responded the Attorney-General. He looked back to the witness.

'Tell this court of the conversation that took place prior to your departure from Gibraltar.'

'There was little discussion,' recalled Deveau. 'Once the *Dei Gratia* was cleared for sailing, it was our responsibility to complete the voyage for which she had been chartered. Captain Morehouse felt he should stay here, as superior officer. And that therefore I should captain the vessel to Italy.'

The Attorney-General was aware of Cochrane suddenly staring up and knew that the judge had also recognised how close Deveau's wording had been to that of Captain Morehouse.

'An attempt, in fact, to *assist* the court?' said the Attorney-General, stressing the disbelief.

'Yes, sir. That is how I understood it.'

'Like discussing your evidence in detail?'

'Sir?'

'There appears often to be great similarity between the evidence of yourself and of others. Has there been much discussion between you?'

'Of course,' said Deveau ingenuously. 'It is not a thing that happens often.'

'Indeed it's not, for which the court should be grateful,' said Flood. 'And during the course of these discussions, there has been agreement about what to say?'

Deveau looked blankly at the other man.

'Have you attempted to get your stories in accord?' persisted Flood.

'No,' said Deveau, at last comprehending.

'So the employment of the same phrases – the same terminology – is a coincidence. Just as finding the *Mary Celeste* upon course was a coincidence … and your finding her, a vessel commanded by a man who had dined the night before departure with Captain Briggs, was a coincidence?'

Deveau shook his head, seeking a response.

'We've told the truth,' he said desperately.

'A statement which many in this court feel is as open to conjecture as is the fate of the unfortunate Captain Briggs and his family,' said Flood, sitting abruptly. He had expected to discompose the man more than he had. But obtaining an open admission had lessened in importance against the evidence of the naval captains. He had maintained the doubt about the salvors' credibility and that mattered.

He became aware of Cochrane's attention and looked up.

'Is there any further evidence you wish to call, Mr Flood?'

The Attorney-General rose, shaking his head.

'I am sufficiently content to lay the facts before Your Lordship,' he said.

'Mr Pisani?'

The salvors' advocate shook his head, but Cornwell rose, seeking permission to speak.

'Mr Cornwell?' allowed Cochrane.

'This hearing has progressed over a great number of days, to the increasing expense of my client, Captain Winchester,' began Cornwell. 'As I had cause to mention at the commencement of this enquiry, it is my client's wish for the *Mary Celeste* to proceed as soon as possible to complete its charter. To that end, there has been brought to this port another captain and crew, a further expenditure. I would now formally seek your decree of restitution of the *Mary Celeste* to him, as rightful owner, upon his payment of a sum into this court sufficient to cover the salvage claim and costs, so that as owner he may discharge his liabilities to the cargo owners … '

The lawyer came to the end of his submission and remained standing, looking hopefully towards the judge.

Cochrane took a long time to respond, flicking back through the large book into which he had made copious notes during the course of the enquiry.

Finally he looked up, his face expressionless.

'I have devoted the greatest attention to Captain Winchester's evidence-in-chief,' he said. 'I have also taken careful note of all the documents and affidavits produced before me. There are certain matters which have been brought to my notice respecting this vessel, my opinion about which I have already very decidedly expressed, and which make it desirable and even necessary that further investigation should take place before the release of the vessel can be considered or before she can quit this port.

'The conduct of the salvors in leaving Gibraltar has, in my opinion, been most reprehensible and may probably influence the decision as to the claim for remuneration for their services. It appears very strange that the captain of the *Dei Gratia*, who knows little or nothing to help the investigation, should have remained here, while the first mate and crew who boarded the *Mary Celeste* and brought her here should have been allowed to go away as they have done. The court will take time to consider the decree for restitution.'

He paused, flicking through his evidence notation again.

'As far as I am aware, Mr Cornwell, this court has not even received from you or from your client documentary proof that he has, in fact, any legal, proprietary right to the *Mary Celeste* ...'

Cornwell twisted to Captain Winchester, sitting just behind him, and there was a hurriedly whispered conversation.

Cornwell returned to the judge.

'My client informs me that, so anxious was he to assist this court and establish his claim to the vessel, he left New York at extremely short notice, omitting unfortunately to arm himself with the particulars of registration and ownership which, of course, his company undoubtedly possesses. He informs me that he will take immediate steps to have those documents forwarded from America and furnished to you ... '

Cornwell hesitated, uncertainly, then continued: 'It is also my duty to acquaint the court of the fact that, so hasty was Captain Winchester's departure, he did not have sufficient time to equip himself with sufficient funds or documents of credit to lay before this court a substantial sum against a claim for salvage. Aware of this oversight, he hopes to arrange a loan from a friend who happens to be in Spain, to enable him to post bond in this court ... '

Cochrane sighed, noisily, looking from Cornwell to the other lawyers and then back again.

'A less patient man than myself might feel his court had been particularly ill-served by the claimants appearing before it ... '

He stopped, looking to the Attorney-General.

'I express myself grateful for the efforts of some to bring cohesion and order to the proceedings. It would seem to me, Mr Cornwell, that your client has some way to go to discharge his duties before there can be any question of restitution.'

He rose, ending the session, and Flood hurried from the court as soon as propriety permitted.

The judge received him fifteen minutes later, hunched reflectively over his desk.

'Confusing business,' he said, as the Attorney-General sat in his usual chair.

'I've brought out everything I can,' said Flood.

'You've done well,' said Cochrane, immediately anxious to deflect any inference of criticism. 'It's still messily unresolved, though.'

The Attorney-General looked curiously at the other man, surprised at the reservation.

'I thought the sea captains were convincing,' he said. 'The surveyor, too.'

'Remarkably so. I'm as convinced as them that something violent took place upon the *Mary Celeste*. The question that I cannot answer is: what?'

'Any news from the constabulary?'

'I gather there's an intention to seek the advice of counsel.'

'I might have expected an approach,' said Flood.

'The feeling was that to obtain such an opinion from you might be embarrassing, engaged as you were in the conduct of the civil proceedings.'

'How long will the opinion take?'

'Not long, I hope,' said the judge. 'There's a limit to the time I can allow before pronouncing upon the decree for restitution. And suspicious though we may be, there is no way I can hold back upon that once we obtain the formal proof of ownership.'

Once again Captain Winchester let the after-court meeting swirl around him, a decision settling in his mind.

'I don't accept that the absence of an ownership certificate is the sole cause for delaying restitution,' said Cornwell. 'Any more than some apparent unhappiness over the mistake with the *Dei Gratia* crew.'

'I wonder if they're attempting another investigation?' said Pisani, as if the thought had just occurred to him.

'There can't be a spar or timber of the *Mary Celeste* that hasn't been scrutinised a dozen times,' said Morehouse wearily.

'There's been no one around the ship for days,' said Winchester. 'I've had Captain Blatchford standing by, ever since he arrived from New York.'

'Another examination of the facts, perhaps,' suggested Pisani, unwilling to give up his idea.

'Criminal?' took up Stokes.

Pisani shrugged, letting the speculation grow.

'It would please the Attorney-General right enough,' said Cornwell. 'He's been conducting a trial for days now.'

'Do you seriously consider there would be grounds for any investigation?' said Stokes, moving against the idea. 'It doesn't seem logical to me.'

'There has been precious little logic at the hearing for a long time,' pointed out Pisani. He looked sadly at the New York owner: 'I'm afraid they're going to keep you on a string for days yet.'

It was a further hour before the meeting broke up. Captain Winchester was the last person to leave the Consul's house.

'As there is a weekend intervening, I thought I'd take a trip to Cadiz to obtain the bail-bond money,' he said. He looked directly at Sprague, intent upon any reaction.

'Probably a good idea,' accepted the American official immediately. 'The court seems minded to inflict upon you whatever delay it can.'

'Is it a lengthy journey?'

169

'Some seventy-five miles or thereabouts,' said Sprague. 'It's a fair road.'

'Then I'll set out at first light,' said the owner.

He ordered a carriage for six but was awake long before dawn. By the time the transport had arrived, he had already packed. He supervised the loading, ensuring that his luggage was out of sight, then sat back in his seat for the slow, winding descent to the peninsula. As they crossed towards the border with the mainland, he looked to his left, trying to isolate the spars and masts of the *Mary Celeste*. He thought he could detect them, but was unsure among so many craft.

The formalities were very brief and Winchester had cleared the colony long before most people were awake. As he began the journey through the gradually widening landscape of Spain, he felt the sense of claustrophobia lift from him; imprisonment must be terrifying, he decided.

The road was better than he had expected and they reached Cadiz by nightfall, Winchester having allowed only the minimum of rest at midday and then paying for an extra set of horses so that they could drive on through the heat.

The brig *Daisy Boynton* was berthed at a sailing jetty, having discharged her cargo. Captain Appleby was aboard, waiting, when Winchester arrived.

'I expected you earlier,' said the younger man.

'I'd have welcomed it being earlier, believe me,' said Winchester.

Appleby put a bottle of local wine at hand for Winchester to replenish his glass when he wanted to, listening without interruption as the owner outlined the enquiry he had been attending.

'Arraign you?' queried the captain, when the older man had come to the end of his account and explained his fears.

'I've little doubt of it.'

'But for what reason?'

'The authorities here are convinced of crime. And seem determined to find a culprit.'

'That's monstrous.'

'It's all of that,' agreed the ship-owner. 'But there appears no appeal.'

'What's your intention?'

'To seek a favour from you,' said Winchester immediately. 'I remembered your destination and hoped you would have discharged. You know me well enough to accept my word as a gentleman, against my paper. I'm asking you to lend me your freight money, so that I can post bond in Gibraltar against the *Mary Celeste* being released. I intend returning it to my agent in the colony by messenger and making my own way to Lisbon, for passage back to America.'

'You're not returning for the conclusion of the hearing?' asked Appleby. The question went beyond surprise, to astonishment.

'I'm *convinced* they intend to arrest me,' he said. 'There are no grounds, but it will take months to obtain a fair hearing and by that time God knows what will have happened to the business in New York. I'm well aware of how bad it will look, but I feel the slur upon my name is a lesser evil than false imprisonment.'

The young man shook his head, doubtfully. Winchester knew he was asking a lot from one so young: Appleby could be little more than twenty-two years of age.

'If you're not inclined to assist, which I shall completely understand, I shall journey on to London and seek protection from the American Ambassador there. It'll need someone in authority to break through the walls they've built for themselves in Gibraltar.'

'You'll provide a Note against the loan?'

'This instant,' said Winchester eagerly. 'Our families have been acquainted for many years. You know well enough there's no risk of my word not being kept.'

Appleby rose and went to a small safe against the bulkhead, near his desk. From it he took a cash box and put it unopened on the table at which Winchester was sitting.

'You're welcome to whatever is there,' he said. 'I'll not sit idly by while a fellow American is hounded by petty officials.'

Winchester counted out the bail-bond money, then wrote out a formal letter of debt and signed it, not putting it into the box but handing it to Appleby. The young man glanced briefly at it, then put it in with the cash that remained.

'You're welcome to passage home aboard the *Daisy Boynton*,' said Appleby.

'It's a generous offer,' said Winchester gratefully. 'But you'll have occasion in the future to call at Gibraltar and I'll do nothing further to involve you with the authorities there. Before I left Gibraltar I took a note of available steamers from the *Maritime Journal*. The *Caledonia* sails from Lisbon on the 6th.'

'Will you raise the matter with Washington when you return?'

'I'll raise it right enough,' vowed the owner. 'And I'll make damned sure there's action taken.'

Winchester dined with Appleby before quitting the *Daisy Boynton*. At the hotel he wrote a long letter to Sprague, informing him of his decision not to return and the following morning had the bail-bond money and the letter put under the seal of the American Consul in Cadiz for transfer to Gibraltar.

By noon he had already taken carriage for the overland route to Portugal. Appleby had been right to be astonished that he was running rather than returning to the colony, reflected Winchester. But only someone who had actually sat in at the hearing day after day and felt the atmosphere build up could appreciate how proper the decision was. Once the ownership certificates arrived it could not affect the eventual release of the *Mary Celeste*. It would cause annoyance, of course, particularly coming so soon after the *Dei Gratia*'s trip to Genoa. But Winchester decided that he couldn't give a damn about annoying Sir James Cochrane or Attorney-General Frederick Solly Flood. He'd asked Consul Sprague to make the contents of his letter clear to both of them, setting out his annoyance at the unfounded accusations and his fear of wrongful arrest. He wanted that to be a warning, an indication that, once back in America, he intended taking every official course open to him to prove them both incompetents and bigots.

He closed his eyes, letting his body move with the motion of the carriage and trying to doze away the fatigue of the previous thirty-six hours.

The enquiry had been a frightening experience, he decided. It would undoubtedly find in favour of the *Dei Gratia*'s salvage claim. But it had failed in the other purpose it had set itself. Despite all the evidence and all the supposition, they were still no nearer learning what had happened to Briggs, his family and crew.

The carriage lurched over an unexpected pot-hole and the owner jerked awake.

And probably, he decided, no one would ever know.

16

More fervently than during any prayers he had uttered since the voyage began, Benjamin Briggs thanked God for the excellence of his crew. Their response was immediate, without the hesitation of bewilderment or the over-haste that would be the prelude to panic. No one shouted. No one ran. What fear there was – and they were all frightened – they hid, not with the self-consciousness that had shown after the sinking of the unknown ship, but because now it would have been a hindrance. It was fortunate that he hadn't adhered absolutely to his father's teaching and given orders only through the mate; there wasn't time for that. Any more than there would have been time to repeat an order; only people who had complete confidence and respect in their captain would have reacted unquestioningly, as these men were doing.

'Abandon ship,' he ordered. He took care to modulate his voice. It was an order no seaman ever wished to hear; the one most likely to affect the control they were all so far showing. So there must be nothing in his voice to increase their anxiety.

'Attempt to ventilate, Mr Richardson.'

'Aye, sir.'

The first mate had already been moving in the direction of the for'ard hatch, anticipating the effort to prevent the explosion that was threatening beneath their feet.

'Fast by the wheel,' he ordered Goodschall.

'Aye, sir.'

'Unship the boat, Mr Gilling.'

Richardson had taken the Lorensen brothers with him to the forward hatch, so the second mate called to Martens as the German emerged from the fo'c'sle, the last to be roused by the activity on deck and the strange rumbling beneath it. Briggs looked apprehensively towards the man. The German paused momentarily at the fo'c'sle head, then moved towards the boat strapped upon its fenders above the main hatch; he walked, not ran, noted the captain.

Briggs turned to the galley mouth, aware of William Head.

'Evacuation supplies,' he said crisply. 'Water, biscuits. As much as you can assemble.'

The steward-cook disappeared without a word into his workplace.

Briggs continued his movement, looking towards the companion-way leading into his cabin. Sarah stood quite calmly at the entrance, waiting her turn to be told what to do. Strange, thought Briggs fleetingly, how his fears of panic had been of the crew, not of his wife. He knew her absolutely, he realised. Sophia had been snatched from her bed and was whimpering at the shocked awakening. His wife had not lingered to dress the child. She had wrapped her first in a shawl, then a coat. Her own hair hung uncollected down her back, but she had hurriedly dressed. It was not until she began to walk towards him that he realised she had forgotten her shoes.

'How serious is it?' she asked. Her voice was almost unnaturally calm; she might have been discussing a rain shower spoiling a Sunday afternoon picnic.

'Bad,' said Briggs, sure of the woman and therefore confident there was no need for false reassurance. 'The cargo is exploding –'

He was stopped by a noise louder than all the others, a screeching, tearing sound like the sort that children sometimes make squeezing the neck of a balloon and then allowing the air to escape. The gas belched up from the hold and, even though he was the farthest away, Briggs recoiled at the smell. Boz Lorensen, who had been standing in front of the hatch, staggered to the rail, retching. He was violently sick before he reached it, his shoulders jerking in spasms. Now there was an opening, the rumblings from the hold were clearer. Even though there was an escape for the gas, there was no lessening of its activity. It continued without a break, a continuous roar, like that of a steam-engine gradually approaching a station.

Richardson and the other Lorensen brother were already at the main hatch, uncoupling the boat.

174

'No time for block and tackle,' said Richardson. 'We'll man-handle her over.'

The four men strained the boat upright, then edged it forward on the fender bar towards the port rail. Boz Lorensen walked unsteadily from the stem of the ship, looking apologetically towards the master. He wedged himself alongside his brother and began shoving.

'Lift on three,' ordered Richardson, beginning to count.

The boat rose up as the men heaved, but Boz Lorensen, still weak, stumbled, upsetting the balance and the metal-edged keel spar sliced down into the rail. The men staggered, but managed to prevent it from falling completely on to the deck.

'Again,' said Richardson, re-counting.

Boz Lorensen got better footing this time and on the second attempt the boat cleared the rail.

'Let it slide,' said Richardson, utilising the axe-like cleft that had been cut into the rail by the boat's bottom.

Richardson held the boat at the rail edge until he was satisfied it would enter the water square, then ordered it in. Volkert Lorensen had the painter and Martens a rope around the stern stay, so that it was held tightly alongside as it splashed down. It was a long drop and there was a surge of water as the boat shipped before rising again.

Briggs had been moving his wife and child towards the boat as his men prepared to cast it over.

'Control of the boat, Mr Richardson,' he said.

The first mate vaulted the rail, then stood to seaward to lift the split rail through which the companion-way was entered when the ship was in port. He took the protesting Sophia from her mother, for the woman to have her hands free to enter the boat, then lowered the child back to her. Sarah sat in the rear, Sophia's head cupped into her shoulder to try to stifle the cries.

Briggs turned inboard, looking at the main hatch they had been prevented from opening by the presence of the boat. It was lashed down, as well as being secured by the fenders upon which the boat had rested. At the very moment he was mentally debating whether he should risk the delay of attempting to remove the hatch, to increase the ventilation, there was another shuddering rumble and a gout of gas, visible because of the dust and debris it carried from the hold, erupted through the already open hatch.

'Collapse the main staysail,' he ordered Gilling and the older Lorensen.

As he hurried to his cabin, fighting against the desire to run, he passed William Head. The cook had joined the handles of two gunny sacks and was tottering along with them over his shoulders, pannier-style.

At the companion-way leading into the cabin, there was a crash and Briggs jerked around, tensed against the edge of the doorway. Gilling and Lorensen had just knocked the shackles free, not bothering to control the descent of the staysail and it had fallen against the stovepipe on the galley roof, splintering it sideways. As the captain watched, the gaff swung from the momentum of the collapse, striking the binnacle. The cleats which had supported it from the decking gave under the blow and the compass smashed out sideways.

Fifteen minutes must have passed since the sound that had first alerted them, Briggs calculated as he entered his cabin. As he did so there was a further eruption beneath his feet, worse than all the others. The deck shuddered so violently that he had to grab out to his desk, to avoid falling.

The for'ard hatch wasn't going to be sufficient, he thought. From the evidence of the build-up so far, there wasn't much time before the eventual explosion and destruction of the vessel. So he would not have time to return again. He thrust the chronometer into his pocket, then snatched up a sextant and navigation book. From a drawer he took the *Mary Celeste*'s papers and register. He tried to pick up the log, but as he did so the sextant began slipping from his grasp, so he abandoned it, deciding that the sighting instrument was more important.

At the cabin door he paused, gazing back. At least his father's failure had been with a shore venture, surroundings in which he was an admitted amateur and for whom sympathy could be felt. He was about to lose a fine ship after less than a month from causes which were well established with such cargo and against which he should have taken better precautions. He turned, peering up the stairs. But what *could* he have done, other than making for another island perhaps a few hours earlier? To have opened the for'ard hatch in the weather they had been experiencing would have been as much bad seamanship as that of which he would now be accused. Those who *knew* wouldn't make the accusation. And he was sure the crew would support him at any subsequent enquiry.

He emerged on deck just as Head was completing the second supply-run from the galley, this time lowering water into the vessel. Goodschall was still at the wheel, obeying orders, although by now the vessel was so becalmed there was hardly any steerage. Boz Lorensen had got into the boat, to stow Head's supplies, and his brother and Martens had led the boat away from amidships and its nearness to the escaping fumes, towards the stern from which they would attach the towline.

'A rope from the lazarette hatch?' queried Gilling, as Briggs hurried towards the boat.

'Yes,' he said, then immediately stopped. A new rope would be stiff and difficult to handle. He turned, seeking an alternative. The main peak halyard, a stout, three-inch-thick rope with one end already spliced to a mainsail gaff was about a foot away.

Gilling was already scrambling into the lazarette, the hatch hastily cast aside.

'The halyard,' called Briggs. 'We'll use the halyard.'

Gilling stopped, with just his head showing from the hatch, then climbed out, pulling the halyard through the tackle blocks and handing the free end to the older Lorensen to make fast to the painter.

The boat looked pitifully small to accommodate them all, thought Briggs, looking down.

'The rafts,' he ordered Gilling, as the man returned from the lazarette. 'Secure them to the boat.'

Unquestioning, the second mate began to unfasten the stays and Volkert Lorensen momentarily let the painter trail while he heaved them over. The young Lorensen took the lines and began paying them out, so that the two rafts were spaced out astern of the lifeboats.

Briggs handed down the articles he had taken from his cabin, gesturing Martens into the boat.

'Secured?' he asked Lorensen.

'Aye,' said the man.

'Into the boat,' said Briggs.

Richardson was standing, holding the boat against the side of the *Mary Celeste*. He handed it back along the deck edge until it was nearly at the stern. The gas convulsions were now so persistent that there was a constant vibration through the vessel and the first mate's hand shook against the decking.

'Getting worse,' said Gilling.

'Into the boat,' said Briggs again.

Fumes were still spurting from the opened hatch, like a volcano without lava. There would be flames and heat soon enough, thought Briggs. There was a sudden sound, not quite an explosion, and a piece of dunnage wood arced like a spear through the hatchway and then disappeared over the bow of the vessel.

'Abandon the wheel,' Briggs ordered Goodschall.

Head made his third return from the galley, with a final gunny sack, and the German stood aside for the cook to enter the boat first. For a moment alone in his ship, Briggs looked around, frowning at the shambles of collapsed sails and the hurry of their departure. The boat-launching had made a bad cut into the rail. Above, the sails still set hung limp and lifeless from the yards.

'It's building up,' warned Richardson, hands still against the deck-edge. 'It's almost shaking me off.'

Reluctantly, Briggs climbed over the rail and got into the boat, giving the halyard a final pull to check its freedom over the pulley. The Lorensen brothers were already at the oars. Behind the boat, the rafts bobbed like chicks following the hen.

'Pull away,' said Briggs.

From the stern came a sob louder than that being made by the child and as he looked up Briggs saw that Sarah had bitten the sound off, lips tightly together, her face close to Sophia's head.

There was another eruption and more stowage material was thrown up. A piece of matting, without the weight of the dunnage wood, drifted leaf-like slowly back and settled gently on the water.

Richardson was pulling constantly at the halyard line, to ensure that no snagging developed on the ship from which they were pulling away. A naturally tidy man, Briggs stacked the things he had taken from his cabin beneath his seat. Head had already stowed the provisions in the rear section, where Sarah sat.

Satisfied that the line was free, Richardson settled himself beside the captain.

'Not a lot of freeboard,' he said, hand against the gunwale.

Briggs looked to starboard. The slack water was less than a foot from the rail edge. He came back into the boat and realised that Richardson had already bailed the water that had been shipped when they had launched from the side of the *Mary Celeste*. He swivelled, looking over Sarah's head. The outline of Santa Maria was smudged on the horizon.

'Safe enough in this water,' he said. 'And the rafts are near to hand.'

Richardson nodded.

Briggs jerked his head towards the landfall.

'Not a good coast,' he said. 'No anchorage worth talking of.'

Richardson frowned, as if the idea of making land had not occurred to him.

'Don't you think she'll clear?' he said, turning back to the half-brig.

'It seemed to be getting worse,' Briggs pointed out. 'Might have been better if we'd got the main hatch off.'

'I'm surprised at the concentration that was there,' said the first mate.

'Rest now,' ordered Briggs.

The Germans stopped rowing, leaning forward against the oars. They were almost three hundred feet from the ship, which was the extent of the halyard, and it dipped only very slightly into the water. Everyone sat silently, waiting and watching the ship. Even Sophia had quietened, caught by the feeling in the boat. It rose very gently in the swell, tiny waves tapping at the hull. Across the water came the empty-belly echo from the deserted ship.

It was almost thirty minutes before Richardson broke the silence.

'If it's going to happen,' he said, 'it's taking long enough.'

'I don't think it's as loud as it was,' said Gilling.

Richardson turned to Briggs, suddenly hopeful.

'Perhaps it's going to be all right,' he said, smiling uncertainly. 'Perhaps the for'ard hatch is going to be sufficient and it's going to ventilate.'

Immediately he received it, the American Consul had considered it his duty to communicate the contents of Captain Winchester's letter to both the Attorney-General and Sir James Cochrane, before the formal reconvening of the enquiry.

Sir James had ordered an adjournment, for Sprague to attempt contacting the New York owner in Cadiz, but the consul there reported that he had already left for Lisbon. It took over a week for a reply to be received from the American authorities in the Portuguese capital and by that time the *Caledonia* had already sailed for America.

Flood had been kept informed of Sprague's efforts to bring Winchester back into the jurisdiction of the court. He set out for the final hearing of the enquiry in greater anticipation than he had all those weeks ago, when it had begun. It had been similar weather then, he remembered, with mist closing off the Peak and the threat of rain later in the day.

Just as he had on that first morning, he strained up as the carriage got near the Governor's residence, able after the almost daily routine to isolate the *Mary Celeste* in harbour.

Flood decided that he had succeeded in the task he had set himself. It *had* been a devilish scheme, as he'd told Sir James that first day. And, to be completely truthful with himself, he had failed to confirm the reason for it. But he'd *pointed* to the motive clearly enough. The attempt to get Deveau from the court had been proof, had any more been needed, that the crew of the *Dei Gratia* were involved in the disappearance of Captain Briggs and his family. Now the departure of Captain Winchester showed where the guilt lay.

He knew that the Board of Trade in London had already

accepted his version of events and passed on to Washington the British government's belief in mutiny and murder. Doubtless they would alert Washington to the owner's flight, so that the authorities would be waiting when he arrived in New York.

The *Gibraltar Chronicle and Commercial Intelligencer* had announced the conclusion of the enquiry and the crowd around the door was greater than it had been on the first day.

Flood had become a celebrity through the hearing. To a degree, he had anticipated the interest that would be shown in British and American newspapers, but had never expected it to extend to the European journals. He had kept a file, containing every mention of the enquiry and the theories that had been advanced; in nearly every report, his name had been prominently mentioned. As he had hoped, the two American newspapers which had conducted personal interviews had accompanied their articles with photographs of him in his official robes.

When his carriage arrived, he recognised four of the journalists who had covered the progress of the enquiry and nodded to them.

'Available for comment afterwards, Mr Attorney-General?'

Flood had not seen who shouted the remark. He looked back to them, nodding again.

'Perhaps,' he said. It would be wrong for him to appear to be courting the public interest.

Baumgartner was waiting just outside the robing room and walked forward to meet the bustling Attorney-General.

'Sir James is anxious to see you before the hearing.'

'I'll robe,' said Flood.

'He said it was urgent ... that you should come immediately,' said the registrar, stopping him.

Shrugging, Flood put his briefcase in the room and then walked behind the court official to the judge's chambers. There was none of the usual cordiality as he entered. Cochrane was at his desk, the ledger into which he had made his notes throughout the hearing open before him.

Flood went to his accustomed chair, without waiting for the judge's invitation.

'I've received the decision of the constabulary,' announced Cochrane.

Flood smiled expectantly. The decision would make a very

dramatic end to the enquiry; the newspaper coverage would be greater than ever. He *would* make a statement to the journalists. The decision would vindicate his beliefs, as they well knew.

'They have decided that there is insufficient evidence to mount a prosecution,' said the judge.

'What!'

Flood half-rose out of his chair, his face open with outrage.

'Insufficient evidence,' repeated the judge. 'There's agreement from every side that cause for suspicion is overwhelming. But the lack of positive evidence to link either Captain Winchester or the *Dei Gratia* crew directly with an attributable crime, even a premeditated motive, makes it too dangerous to mount a prosecution.'

'*I* would have prosecuted,' said Flood, still unable to keep the incredulity from his voice.

'I'm aware you would ... so are the authorities.'

'Then I should surely be allowed to proceed, in a criminal court.'

'Not if the police here are unprepared to make a case. And counsel's advice is that if we arraigned any one of the people who have appeared before us at the enquiry, then their defence lawyers would destroy any case we were able to bring.'

'But what about the flight of Captain Winchester?'

'It proves –'

'Guilt,' insisted Flood. 'What other reason would he have had for fleeing, unless he were frightened of what was to be uncovered?'

'It would make a very strong piece of *circumstantial* evidence, if only there were something positive to link the man with crime ... insurance fraud, for instance. Just one thing – that's all we need.'

The full extent of what he was being told registered with Flood. He rose, walking to the window overlooking the bay. The disbelief numbed him.

'It means that a crime has been committed ... and that we are probably letting the guilty men escape justice.'

'I've made that point,' said Cochrane.

'Is a full report being made to London?'

'Of course.'

'They could overrule the decision here.'

183

'The final decision *came* from London, because I protested against its being made locally.'

'*London* say no proceedings?'

'Yes.'

'But they've accepted my view, of murder and mutiny. Alerted the American government, even.'

'I know. And for good purpose. If there were mutiny and somewhere one of the crew is located, then we've got our positive proof. We're not closing the door to prosecution by deciding against moving now.'

But he'd *wanted* it pursued now, while everyone except Winchester was in the colony and easily apprehended. He'd *wanted* to be involved.

'What chance will there be of bringing all these people together in six months' time!' he demanded, exasperated. 'They'll have disappeared to God knows where.'

'I'm not unaware of the difficulties,' said Cochrane, irritated at the apparent blame the Attorney-General was attaching to him for the decision.

'It's unbelievable,' said Flood, making angry patting gestures against the window sill. 'Utterly unbelievable.'

He turned into the room again:

'The *Mary Celeste* crew were German, with families. I'm going to communicate the whole affair to the Prussian authorities and ask them to be on the look-out for anyone answering the descriptions we can provide. There'll be a time when they will want to come out of hiding and return home ... '

'It could do no harm,' said the judge doubtfully.

Flood returned to his chair, sitting forward upon it and looking directly at the other man.

'I regard this as a personal failure,' he said.

'There's no reason why you should,' said Cochrane immediately. 'I know of no one else who would have worked as hard as you have.'

'I'm *convinced* I'm right,' said the Attorney-General, unwilling even now to concede that the affair was going to end without any action. 'There are too many inconsistencies in the story for it to go unchallenged.'

'I know the doubts, as well as you,' said Cochrane sadly.

'Then what are we to do?'

'There's little we can do,' said the judge. 'I intend making my feelings as clear as possible.'

There was a hesitant sound at the door and Baumgartner appeared. Cochrane rose, dismissively, and the Attorney-General hurried back to his robing room. He felt robbed, as defiled as he would have been had he returned home to find his house forcibly entered and the objects he had accumulated over a lifetime stolen for ever. It was a preposterous decision not to institute proceedings. And even more preposterous that there was no one to whom he could appeal against it.

He stumped into court, ignoring the formal greetings of acknowledgment from the lawyers who were already assembled. Sprague sat slightly apart and gave no awareness of the Attorney-General's entry. In the first row of seats behind the lawyers the captain and first mate of the *Dei Gratia* sat side by side.

Cochrane entered almost immediately and like Flood ignored the customary greetings from the assembled lawyers:

'Before making any pronouncement upon this claim, I wish to call before me the American Consul to this colony, Mr Horatio Sprague ... and also Mr Cornwell.'

The men rose immediately to their feet, as if in expectation of the summons. They moved with slight uncertainty towards the witness area, but the judge stopped them, indicating a position in the centre of the court, directly below where he sat.

Looking beyond Sprague and Cornwell, to the lawyers, Cochrane said: 'It is proper that you gentlemen should know the reason for the somewhat lengthier adjournment than you were first asked to accept because of the failure of Captain Winchester to provide either bail-bond or certificates of ownership of the *Mary Celeste* –'

Reminded, the judge reached sideways, picking up a document. 'A delay, incidentally, which has enabled the ownership document to arrive by steamer from New York.'

He looked back to the court.

'On the evening of the adjournment, it is known that Captain Winchester left this colony for Spain, ostensibly to raise funds from friends and acquaintances with whom he was in contact there. It was subsequently brought to my notice that this was not the only intention of Captain Winchester in leaving the jurisdiction of this court. From Spain, Captain Winchester, without the knowledge or permission of this court, travelled to Lisbon and from there took passage upon a steamer for New York.'

It was obvious that the lawyers and the *Dei Gratia* crew knew of Winchester's flight. There was not the slightest expression of surprise from anyone.

Cochrane stared down at the two men before him.

'I feel this court deserves some statement from you two gentlemen, closely involved as you were during his stay in Gibraltar with Captain Winchester – '

'I must ask the court to accept my complete assurance that at no time was I aware of Captain Winchester's intention not to return,' responded Cornwell immediately. 'In fact, I was unaware until several days afterwards that he had even gone into Spain. Had I had the slightest awareness of Captain Winchester's plans, then I must assure Your Lordship and this court that I would have taken every effort to dissuade Captain Winchester from embarking upon the course he did.'

The judge hesitated for several moments, then said, 'A fulsome explanation, Mr Cornwell. And one which this court accepts.'

He turned to the Consul.

'Mr Sprague?'

'I would also like to assure this court that I had not the slightest knowledge that Captain Winchester might not return,' said the Consul. 'Before he left, he told me he was going to Cadiz. He knew people there from whom he felt he could raise the bail-bond. I inferred from the way that he spoke that his sole reason for making this journey was to expedite the hearing before this court ... '

Sprague paused, the defence appearing prepared.

'Like Mr Cornwell, had I even suspected that it was not Captain Winchester's intention to return, then I would have done everything to persuade him against such a thing.'

'Yet it was you to whom he wrote?' said the judge, making the doubt obvious.

'The letter was the first intimation I had that he would not be coming back. It accompanied money sufficient for the bond.'

'What reason did Captain Winchester give for fleeing?' demanded the judge.

The question surprised the Consul. He frowned, unsure what response the man wanted.

'I have already communicated the letter to you, My Lord ... ' he said doubtfully.

'And I believe that others in this court as inconvenienced as I have been should have the benefit of that information,' said Cochrane.

'Captain Winchester said he feared arrest,' said Sprague quietly.

'Arrest?' prompted the judge.

'From the letter it appears that Captain Winchester believed he was suspected by this court of certain involvement in the disappearance from the *Mary Celeste* of some if not all of the crew. He describes the suppositions as preposterous, but says that, so strong did he detect the suspicion to be, he felt it would be impossible for the matter to be fairly considered — '

'So he ran away?'

'He insists that he is a completely innocent man whose continued presence here was achieving nothing. He did not leave without ensuring that he had complied with every request made to him by the court.'

Cochrane's demand that the contents of the letter be made public had initially surprised the Attorney-General as greatly as it had startled the American Consul, but now Flood appreciated the move. Such a protracted discussion would guarantee lengthy coverage from the journalists outside, at least three of whom were employed by New York publications. The judge was apparently determined that Winchester should not escape the suspicion and condemnation of the court, even if he had slipped away from its control.

'Has it been your awareness in the past, Mr Sprague, that *innocent* men fear courts of law?' demanded the judge.

The Consul shifted uncomfortably:

'No, My Lord.'

'Is it not normally the reaction of guilty men?'

'Yes, My Lord.'

'Was Captain Winchester not aware that this was a properly

187

convened court under the jurisdiction of Her Majesty, the Queen of England?'

'He was aware of that,' said Sprague, his discomfort increasing.

'And that British jurisprudence has formed the basis for every judicial system in the world?'

'That is accepted, My Lord.'

'So Captain Winchester, a completely innocent man, saw fit to flee a system recognised throughout the world as the fairest that exists?'

'I do not think Captain Winchester considered the matter as deeply as that,' said Sprague helplessly.

'What do you think Captain Winchester *did* consider?' pressed the judge.

'He felt ... ' started Sprague, then stopped, realising the risk of impertinence if not contempt in what Winchester had asked him to say. 'I feel that Captain Winchester acted hastily, without properly considering the fullest implications of his actions,' he resumed. Admittedly at a low level, his function was nevertheless supposed to be that of a diplomat: and nothing could be achieved by enraging the judge further. 'He hastily came to the conclusion that he would be inveigled into a situation from which it would be difficult to extricate himself without considerable loss of time. He is adamant that his only function in coming here was to assist the court in its findings and to reclaim the *Mary Celeste* as its rightful, principal owner. I know he would be deeply distressed at the thought that his actions could be construed as indicating any involvement or culpability in the strange matters that have been occupying this court for the past weeks ... '

'What other interpretation do you imagine that there is, Mr Sprague?' persisted Cochrane relentlessly.

'As I have attempted to indicate,' said the Consul, 'it was the hasty action of a man not properly considering the outcome ... '

Sprague decided that he was doing badly.

'I have often had occasion to define a crime as the hasty action of a man not properly considering the outcome,' said the judge.

'I can only repeat Captain Winchester's letter to me, in which he resisted such a verdict in the strongest possible terms.'

'I want the fullest account of the court's annoyance over what has happened transmitted to your government in Washington,' said Cochrane. 'I further intend through the diplomatic means open to me in my own country to inform the American authorities of my severe disapproval of Captain Winchester's conduct. I do not consider that the behaviour we have witnessed from Captain Winchester can be the behaviour of an innocent man and were this a criminal rather than a civil court, greater powers than this court possesses would be invoked to obtain from Captain Winchester a fuller explanation.'

'I assure this court that I will communicate its views to the appropriate department in Washington,' undertook Sprague.

Cochrane nodded, dismissing both consul and lawyer, then straightened at the bench. Briefly his gaze met that of the Attorney-General, but Flood kept his face free of any expression of approval at the man's outspokenness. The congratulations could come later. Swingeing though the comments had been, the fact remained that the matter was beginning and ending as a civil matter, while they well knew a crime was involved.

'It is now my function,' began the judge, 'to turn to the purpose for which this court was convened, to adjudicate upon the claim for salvage entered by the captain and crew of the British brigantine *Dei Gratia*.' As was the normal custom, Cochrane had written out his formal judgment and every few moments his eyes dropped to his prepared statement.

'Within the last few minutes, you have heard me express the court's strongest disapprobation of the behaviour of Captain Winchester.'

He stopped, looking to see if Sprague were taking a note of what he was saying. A notebook lay open upon the table in front of the American Consul.

'It is my intention to continue to express displeasure, this time with people who at least showed sufficient responsibility to remain in court for the adjudication. This enquiry takes the gravest view of the action of the *Dei Gratia* master, Captain David Reed Morehouse, in despatching from the jurisdiction of this court his first mate, whose continued presence was considered vital to a satisfactory conclusion of this case, being as he was the person most concerned with the salvage of the *Mary Celeste* ... '

Briefly his eyes dropped to his judgment: ' ... it is the feeling of this court that despite every attempt and effort on the part of counsel present, there remain a large number of unanswered questions regarding this matter. Whether those questions will ever be satisfactorily explained can only be a matter of conjecture. I consider I would be failing in my duties as adjudicator of these events if, however, I ignored those unanswered questions and the suspicions to which they give rise in any enquiring, investigative mind.'

Coming to the vital section of his pronouncement, Cochrane was staring directly at the *Dei Gratia* captain and mate. The men looked strangely similar, beards spread before them, hands held against their knees, both frowning slightly in their anxiety fully to comprehend what the man was saying.

'Early in this hearing,' Cochrane continued, 'it was established that the aggregate value of the cargo and hull of the *Mary Celeste* was in the region of $51,000. It was further established, I believe in a reply to a question from the Attorney-General, that although every case has to be judged upon its individual merits, as this case is certainly being judged, there is in maritime circles an anticipation of salvage awards. Sometimes, bearing in mind the hazards to which salvors go to bring an empty vessel safely to port, that award can be as high as 40 per cent ... '

Flood was regarding Oliver Deveau as the judge spoke. Fleetingly, a smile flickered over the first mate's face.

'Counsel acting for the claimants in this case have argued eloquently of the difficulty of the *Dei Gratia*, with a cargo of petroleum, reducing its crew from eight to five to bring a derelict six hundred miles from where it was found to port here, in Gibraltar.'

He stopped, preparing them for something of importance:

'That there were hazards out there, off the Azores, has been argued equally eloquently by the Attorney-General.'

Deveau's smile had gone now, replaced by an even deeper frown than before.

'It is my intention to award to the captain and crew of the *Dei Gratia* the sum of £1,700, which, translated into American currency for the sake of comparison against aggregate value, is $8,300.'

Cochrane stopped again, this time for the smallness of the amount to be assimilated by those in court. Pisani had twisted to his client, abruptly shaking his head to some point that Captain Morehouse had leaned forward to make. The *Dei Gratia*'s master's face was flushed and his always staring eyes seemed even more prominent in his head.

'I further order that the costs of this case should be paid out of the property salved ... '

Cochrane paused, looking over to the American Consul: 'A fact which I entrust you to bring not only to Captain Winchester's attention, but also to that of the American authorities to whom you are going to express my displeasure – '

Sprague half rose, nodding.

'It is also my intention,' resumed the judge, 'to make an order that the cost of expert witnesses' examination and analysis of the decking, hull and other articles aboard the *Mary Celeste* shall be charged against the $8,300 I have awarded to the salvors.'

Cochrane concluded his judgment and the court was suddenly hushed, no one immediately realising that he had finished. The awareness came as he rose to leave the chamber. Before he had got out of the room, Captain Morehouse was at the lawyers' bench angrily pulling Pisani around.

The Attorney-General knew there were some formalities to be completed in his chambers with the court registrar and was not surprised that the summons to join the judge took longer than usual.

This time Cochrane poured sherry, handing Flood a glass as he entered: 'Pisani has told Baumgartner he intends to appeal,' he said.

'He can't,' said Flood.

'I know. That's what Baumgartner told him.'

'What did he say to that?'

'Called it a travesty of justice.'

'If there's been a travesty of justice, it's not from this quarter,' said Flood positively.

'It was the best I could do, in the circumstances,' said Cochrane.

'It was far more than I expected you to do,' said Flood. 'No one can be left in any doubt, after a judgment like that.'

'I didn't intend them to be.'

'It *will* be virtually impossible to arrest them, if a member of the *Mary Celeste* crew ever does reappear,' said Flood bitterly.

'I know.'
'So this will be the end of it?'
'I would expect so.'
'So we'll never know.'
'Know?'
'What really happened on the *Mary Celeste*.'

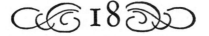

For more than an hour they had remained in the boat, their hopes rising and falling almost as frequently as the tiny vessel lifted and fell upon the gentle swell. Once, about thirty minutes after they had abandoned her, the sounds had died almost completely from inside the *Mary Celeste* and Captain Briggs had been upon the point of ordering a return to the ship when there was that sudden train-into-the-station sound and then more dunnage was spewed from the for'ard hold as a fresh build-up of gas and fumes was expelled.

There was virtually no wind now, so that what movement there was came from the current. Briggs had deputed Gilling to watch their drift and twice the second mate had had to put the Lorensen brothers to the oars, to maintain the distance between the lighter, more easily carried boat and the heavier ship.

As unashamedly as he prayed before and after each meal in whatever company he might find himself, Briggs had led a prayer meeting in the becalmed craft. There was eagerness in the way the men had joined in, sitting with heads bowed, following him loudly in common prayer and then remaining in the attitude of devotion, their lips moving slightly as each begged silently for the danger to pass.

The baby recovered from her fright towards the end of the prayers, curious as to why everyone was behaving so oddly. The period of enjoyment of a new experience in such a small craft soon passed and then she became fractious at the restrictions upon her movement. Arien Martens had very early tried to shift position, ironically to give the boat a better balance, and water had shipped in even though the movement had been very slight. Briggs briefly thought of putting some men aboard one of the rafts, deciding almost immediately against it. Instead he ordered that everyone remain where they sat.

By nine-thirty it had become almost oppressively hot, reminiscent of the thunderstorms of which they had first thought they were victims, before realising it was the cargo sounding. The cook had ladled from his ample supply of water, handing the cup first to the woman and child, next to the captain and then down through order of seniority. Sophia had complained of hunger and grimaced at the ship's biscuit that was handed to her. She started to whimper, but Sarah quietened her and eventually she sat gnawing upon it, the activity taking her mind off having to be cramped constantly upon her mother's lap.

'The drift is away from land,' Gilling reported. Towlines to the rafts were submerged beneath the water.

'I know,' said Briggs.

The sound from the vessel was taking a long time to clear, but increasingly Briggs was beginning to feel Richardson's optimism. Had he kept them aboard for only a few minutes longer, to release the main hatch, the ship would have been safe by now, he realised. But there was no way he could have known that. So the decision to abandon had been the correct one.

'Don't reckon we'll be needing a landfall,' said Richardson.

'I hope we don't have to attempt that one,' said Briggs, jerking over his shoulder. He stayed twisted around, looking at his wife. She smiled at him, a hopeful expression. She was still very frightened, he recognised. But not so much as when they had first had to leave the ship. He smiled back.

'It's going to be all right,' he mouthed.

'I know,' she said back, silently.

'Make a story to tell,' said Richardson.

'One I'd have gladly avoided,' said Briggs, with feeling, turning back to stare at his empty ship.

The boat lifted suddenly, higher than it had been, and Briggs looked outboard curiously, wondering at the change of current.

'Binnacle won't take a moment to repair,' said Richardson, who had seen the gaff knock it off its mountings. 'The cleats have gone adrift, that's all.'

'Galley chimney might take a little longer,' said Gilling.

Briggs knew that beneath the matter-of-factness of the conversation there was the need for them to convince themselves that they would soon be returning to the ship.

'Work of an hour or more, that's all,' he said briskly. Hadn't one of his father's early teachings been the importance of instilling confidence?

'Known this happen before, with a cargo of alcohol,' said Martens. 'Coaster I piloted in Hamburg. There'd been some rumbling, but they hadn't realised what it was. When the explosion came, it blew the hatch right off, breaking the mate's arm. There was so much dust and debris that they thought they were on fire and almost abandoned ship before they realised what had happened.'

'They stayed aboard?' demanded Volkert Lorensen.

'It was a small cargo. And a shorter journey than ours. One blow and it was over.'

'I wish to God this one would soon end,' said Gilling. It was a sincere expression, not a blasphemy.

The *Mary Celeste* was growing quiet again. Only occasionally did anything reach them, a sound like the snoring of a grumpy old man.

'It *must* be clear now,' said Richardson.

'We'll give it a little longer,' said Briggs cautiously. Having come so near to disaster, it would be ridiculous to take any further chances.

'Anyone hungry?' asked Head, from behind.

No one accepted.

'We'll repair your smoke-stack in time for dinner,' promised Richardson. It was an attempt at lightness, but there was no laughter.

Water splashed over the side, no more than a few droplets, and Volkert Lorensen played the boat around with his oar, bringing it into the current.

'Over two hours now,' said Richardson, looking up professionally towards the sun. The sky wasn't as clear as it had been. Flat, formless clouds were spreading lightly across, like a skein of muslin.

'Seems much longer,' said Gilling.

The Lorensen brothers looked towards Briggs, anticipating the order.

The eruption from the ship was the worst there had been. The whole vessel seemed to shiver under its force and small waves began rippling out from the hull, where it actually moved in the water. Sophia cried out, frightened. There was a second, slightly less violent than the first and the sails that were still set flickered under the outrush of gas. The *Mary Celeste* moved slightly, putting the boat a little to port of the stern. That time there hadn't been any dunnage or debris thrown out, Briggs realised. Another like that and there would surely be an explosion in the hold; he wondered if the timbers had been stretched already, so that the ship would be taking water. Unless it were a bad breach, the pumps would be adequate, once they got back on board.

This time the sound did not diminish, but maintained an ugly, throat-clearing cough and the waves created by the explosion caught the boat, lifting it in a series of tiny jogging motions and more water was shipped. Unasked, Goodschall picked up the bail and began tossing the water from the craft.

'Benjamin!'

Everyone turned, seized by the despair in Sarah's voice. Sophia had demanded to go to the toilet and the woman was holding the child over the stern of the vessel, so that she was facing back towards the distant outline of Santa Maria. The landfall was almost concealed now, swamped by a great shroud of oil-black clouds that were seeping towards them, so low that in places they almost appeared to be touching the water. Ahead of the clouds came the rain, a fierce, scudding downpour so forceful that it was flattening the sea like metal under a tinsmith's hammer. And then there was the first of the wind, feeling out for them like cold hands, fighting the rain for a chance to whip the water up.

'Oh, my God!' said Richardson, careless of any offence he might cause the captain.

Briggs turned as the first of the rain swept over them, with the suddenness of a swab bucket being thrown into the boat, gazing towards the ship. There was thunder with the squall, making it impossible to calculate which sound was coming from the atmosphere above and which emanated from the *Mary Celeste*.

'She's sails set,' he said, quietly, in horrified realisation. 'She'll run from us.'

'Oh, God!' said Richardson, again. This time there was anguish in his voice.

'Haul for the ship,' ordered Briggs urgently.

The Lorensen brothers started rowing immediately, aware of what could happen.

The wind was stronger now, churning the waves. Gilling snatched the cup from where the cook was sitting and began scooping the water from beneath their feet in almost timed motion with Goodschall, the movement becoming faster as the sea started gushing over the gunwales. The baby was crying and when Briggs looked back he saw that Sarah had at last broken down, clamping her lips against the sound but with her shoulders pumping with her tears.

'The line, Mr Richardson,' he said to the mate. 'See if you can haul us with the line.'

Richardson clambered to the bow, the movement bringing in more sea, and tried to help the rowers by dragging the boat along its own towline. The rope was wet and heavy and to have given it a chance to work, he would have had to stand with his feet braced against the prow, so that the stem would have been actually forced beneath the water.

They were still about two hundred and fifty feet from the *Mary Celeste*, completely engulfed in the storm, when the first wind reached the ship. She seemed to start, like a nervous horse suddenly surprised by the approach of a rider. The jib and fore-topmost staysail responded first, slapping and cracking against the yards.

'Row!' urged Briggs, leaning forward to encourage the men. 'The sails are filling. Row!'

'The rafts,' shouted Gilling. 'They are dragging at us.'

Briggs hesitated, realising the importance of the decision. Regaining the ship was the only consideration, he judged. And they still had a chance of doing that.

'Cut them adrift,' he said.

For the first time, there was a discernible hesitation at an order. Then Gilling untied the towline to the rafts. Almost immediately, the rowers appeared to achieve more speed.

Briggs strained through the storm-gloom, intent upon the other sails set upon the *Mary Celeste*.

The foresail still drooped but the upper and lower topsails were gradually moving.

'Less than two hundred feet now, lads,' encouraged Richardson.

The two Germans were straining at the oars, eyes bulged and the veins in their faces and necks knotted starkly against their skin. They had got into a regular metronome movement, breath grunting from them. Briggs could see that they were almost exhausted. To exchange with Goodschall and Martens would be time-wasting. The line was no longer taut between them and the boat. It was almost completely submerged, just occasionally visible, curled and flaccid, just below the surface.

The jib filled completely and the stem of the *Mary Celeste* came up, making the long bowsprit shift in a curious, seeking movement, like a dog sniffing a scent.

'She'll move soon,' warned Richardson.

There was a great deal of water in the boat now. It lapped just below the seats, so that they sat with their feet and legs submerged almost to their knees. Sarah had the baby pulled protectively from her lap and clenched against her chest. Her eyes were closed and her lips were moving in constant prayer.

The Lorensen brothers were flagging, their rowing going out of time, the boat so heavy it was hardly making any way. He would have to change, Briggs knew.

'Goodschall, Martens,' he said. There was immediate comprehension. The Lorensens stopped, in unison, and flopped backwards, eyes glazed with near-unconsciousness, just pulling their legs over the seat for the other two Germans to take their places. The new men started with renewed fervency and the boat appeared to move faster through the water.

'She's picking up,' reported Richardson from the prow and for the briefest moment Briggs thought the mate was talking about the craft they were in. Then he looked towards the *Mary Celeste*.

The sails would never fill completely because she was moving without a helmsman, but the foresail was stretched, together with the upper and lower topsails. Slowly at first, almost as if unwilling, but then gradually with increasing speed the *Mary Celeste* began to pick up.

'Row, damn you! Row!' pleaded Richardson.

Goodschall and Martens were making an incredible effort, oar blades falling and rising, but the distance between them and the ship was becoming visibly greater.

Because he was in the prow, Richardson was the first to realise that the rope that had been lost to sight was gradually emerging from the water again as the gap lengthened, like an obscene taunt at how far away they still were.

'She'll drag us,' shouted Briggs.

Almost immediately the tow rope twanged tight and there was a shudder through the boat. It surged forward, achieving the sort of speed the seamen had been trying to attain, and they stopped, twisting curiously around.

'In the stern. Get the weight in the stern,' ordered Briggs, foreseeing the fresh danger. The men scrambled towards the woman, baby and stores, trying to bring the nose up. The two Lorensen brothers flopped completely in the bottom of the boat, only their heads and shoulders clear of the water, supported against the legs of Martens. He squatted over them, chaffing their heads and necks, trying to get some response from them.

'She'll yaw soon,' predicted Richardson. 'She can't run on for ever.'

'We're being pulled away from Santa Maria,' said Briggs.

'So near,' moaned Richardson. 'We were so near.'

'This wind will be scouring her holds,' said Briggs, seeing the irony. 'Making her safe.'

He eased around in the crush of people. Sarah still sat with her eyes pressed tight, unwilling to witness what was happening, her mouth twitching in perpetual prayer. She had completely enveloped the child in her protective clothing, so that only a small part of her face was visible. Sophia was trying to press closer to her mother, eyes blank and unseeing with fear. She was making no sounds, but spasms were jerking her tiny body, as if she were fevered. It would be terror, Briggs knew.

He felt out, touching his wife's shoulder, and she opened her eyes.

'You're going to save us, aren't you, Benjamin? It will be all right?' she demanded. For the first time that he could ever recall in their married life, there was something like an accusation in her voice.

'I don't know,' he said, honest even now.

'I don't want to die!' she blurted. 'I don't want Sophia to die.'

'The nose is going down,' said Gilling, fear showing at last.

The rope connecting them to the *Mary Celeste* was so rigidly stretched that it could have been a piece of metal. And as relentlessly as a steel bar, it was pushing down against their stem, thrusting it lower and lower, so that the wind-driven waves were pouring in, every fresh gush of water bringing them nearer to becoming completely swamped.

'Cut the line,' said Briggs.

There was a hesitation when they realised that there was no axe aboard the boat. It was Gilling who produced the clasp knife, spluttering forward through the water and starting to saw at the painter. The water kept forcing him back, so that he constantly lost the spot against which he was trying to cut, and then suddenly, as abruptly as they had spurted forward, their crazy careering stopped.

'Snapped,' said Richardson. 'It snapped somewhere on the ship.'

The waterlogged boat wallowed in the waves, hardly any freeboard remaining. Before anyone could prevent it happening, one of the seats was lifted out by the force of the water and floated free.

He didn't know if he could do what Sarah wanted, Briggs thought suddenly. He didn't know if he could keep her alive. Or any of them. Angrily he cast the thought aside. The despair which had momentarily gripped him and which he knew held the others was almost as dangerous as their predicament, he realised. With the need for the stern weight gone, he shifted back amidships, shouting the orders. The Lorensen brothers were recovering, he saw gratefully.

'Raise the sail,' he said. 'We'll set course for Santa Maria. Everyone who can, bail.'

Briggs stared back to the heaving water, seeking the life-rafts he now recognised it had been a mistake to abandon.

Richardson and Martens started trying to erect a canvas. Gilling and Goodschall continued with the bailing and the Lorensen brothers stirred. Without any utensils, they slumped in the boats on their haunches, trying to scoop the water back over the sides with their cupped hands. William Head had taken off his reefer jacket and tried to cover Sarah and Sophia with it, Briggs saw. As he looked, the cook began searching for a canister, then dropped into the boat and started to use his hands, like the two Germans. It was difficult to make any distinction between the sea and the gunwales, so deeply was the boat awash. Briggs was trying to bail now, jerking his hands in the sort of splashing movements he'd used the previous year, when they had taken Arthur to the beach at Cape Cod. It had been fun then.

'No good,' gasped Head. 'It's no good.'

Briggs paused, to stare out to sea. The *Mary Celeste* was bent fully into the wind, all her sails seeming full. Then a cloud thicker than the rest swept down and she was lost for the last time.

'Weight,' shouted Briggs, to the cook. 'There's too much weight. Throw the food over.'

Obediently, the man heaved the gunny sacks from the boat. They scarcely cleared the water as he put them over the side. The boat did not appear to rise at all.

Richardson and Martens managed a stud-sail of sorts, trying to get some wind, but the gusts eddied around them, with little direction. The waves were very high now, lurching towards them in great walls of water, and the boat didn't lift, so that they were completely washed over. Boz Lorensen, emptied by his efforts to row, was the first to go, yelling as he felt himself lifted by a wave and stretching out his hand, which incredibly his brother snatched out and grabbed, preventing him from being carried completely away. He was pushed outside the boat, though, which lifted slightly. For a moment Volkert stayed inboard, pulling his brother to where he could get a grip on the gunwale, then looked towards the woman and child in the rear of the vessel. Without a word, he edged over, putting his body alongside his brother and reaching over, so that one of his arms was over the man's shoulders, supporting him.

'It's going up,' said Briggs, knowing there was excitement in his voice, but uncaring. 'The boat is going up.'

Martens was the next over, trying a grip on the side opposite from the brothers, professionally knowing that if she continued to rise in the water they would need to balance.

He shouted to Goodschall in German and the young man hesitated, then slipped over, so that there were two men on either side of the boat. In the troughs beneath the waves, it was just possible to see the edge of the boat. Gilling, Richardson and Head were on their hands and knees, bailing with the ferocity of men who knew there was little hope left but refused to believe it. Briggs tried to trim the stud, seeking the wind.

Richardson sat back upon his heels, nearing collapse, gazing dully up at the captain and the sail he was trying to control.

Awareness suddenly came into his face and he said, 'North-west.'

Briggs turned to him.

'The wind,' said the first mate, limply trying to indicate the sail. 'It's north-west. To get us to Santa Maria, it would have to be south-westerly.'

The man was right, realised Briggs, feeling the hope seep from him.

Now that the wind was set into a quarter, it built up the waves even higher, so that there was no interval in the seas that engulfed them. The weakest of them all, Boz Lorensen, released his hand-hold first, and trying to save him a second time Volkert let go and they were carried away together, the older man still attempting to keep his brother's head clear of the water, even though they had been separated from the only thing that could possibly save them. Briggs was tearing at the stud, to bring it down, knowing it had become a greater danger than help, straining through the rain and clouds in an effort to see Santa Maria. There was nothing, just sea and rain and blackness. With no way to keep her into the running sea, the next wave caught the boat broadside, tipping her up and tearing the gunwales from Martens and Goodschall. As quickly as she had lifted, the boat fell away again and there was the dull, slapping sound as the hull came down upon the two men beneath. The blood smeared out and Sarah screamed, an hysterical sound. Neither of the bodies surfaced.

The boat corkscrewed as it came down, throwing them all off-balance, and then in an immediate rush of water Richardson suddenly wasn't there any more. Briggs came around at the cry for help. As he had been hurled from the boat, Richardson had grabbed out, snatching at the cook's arm and pulling him overboard as well. Briggs saw them once, and then a wall of water engulfed them and they did not come up. Something else lifted on the waves and Briggs recognised one of the rafts.

'Make for the raft,' he shouted, to the men he couldn't see. 'There's a raft on the port quarter.'

'The baby!' Sarah suddenly shouted.

She was holding Sophia out towards Briggs, imploringly. The little bundle sagged limply and Briggs realised that, as she had crouched trying to hold the baby against her, Sarah had actually held the baby's head beneath the water.

He snatched the child, before the woman had a chance to pull at the protective covering to discover what she had done.

'It's all right,' he said. 'She's all right.'

It was the first lie he had ever told her.

Sarah suddenly stood up, eyes staring in her hysteria. Gilling grabbed out, to bring her down, so the inrush of water caught him first, lifting him and carrying him bodily into the woman, knocking her backwards over the stern. For a moment they surfaced, about a yard apart. Briggs fell into the stern, reaching out for her and momentarily she stretched her hand towards his, trying to grasp at his groping fingers; and then she went under and he never saw her again.

He still had the baby in his left arm, holding her roughly. He turned, feeling beneath the water for the stern-seat, and then sat with the lifeless bundle in his arms, clutched high against him, the clothes raised around her again, to keep the water off.

He never saw the wave, but was aware of its movement, lifting him from the boat like a giant hand; and then he knew he was going under water and that his heavy clothes were dragging him down. He tightened his grasp upon Sophia.

Everything else had gone. But it wouldn't take her. He'd promised Sarah it wouldn't take the baby.

Epilogue

Could this have been the fate of the *Mary Celeste* and the people aboard?

It was the conviction held, in varying degrees, by nearly everyone most closely involved in the mystery.

In 1886, Captain Winchester told a friend:

> The cause of the hurried stoppage of the vessel, of the launching of the boat and of the abandonment was, in my opinion, that the alcohol which formed her cargo being in these red-oak barrels, a wood which is extremely porous, enough of its fumes exhaled through the pores of the wood to mingle with the foul air of the hold and generate an explosive gas which blew off the fore-hatch.
>
> Believing that she was on fire below and considering the inflammable nature of her cargo and mindful of the fact that his wife and child were on board, Captain Briggs, on the spur of the moment, resolved to heave the vessel to, launch the longboat, get into it and remain at a safe distance from the brig awaiting further developments. This was probably done, but the brig's mainsail being stowed, she had no after-sail to keep her to the wind and she got stern away and backed off until the wind filled her topsail when, like a frightened deer, away she went, leaving her crew behind.

It was a theory supported by Captain Henry Appleby, the man who in Cadiz loaned Winchester the bail-bond money to retrieve his vessel. A minor explosion actually happened aboard Captain Appleby's *Daisy Boynton*, with a cargo of alcohol en route for Bilbao, in northern Spain.

And it was the conclusion reached after an exhaustive investigation by Dr Oliver Cobb, of Easthampton, Massachusetts, a cousin of both Captain Briggs and his wife, who was Sarah Elizabeth Cobb before her marriage.

Said Dr Cobb:

I think that the cargo of alcohol, having been loaded in cold weather at New York, early in November and the vessel having crossed the Gulf Stream and being now in comparatively warm weather, there may have been some leakage and gas may have accumulated in the hold. The captain, having care for his wife and daughter, was probably unjustifiably alarmed and, fearing a fire or an explosion, determined to take his people in the boat away from the vessel until the immediate danger should pass ... whatever happened, it is evident that the boat, with ten people in her, left the vessel and that the peak halyard was taken as a tow line and as a means of bringing the boat back to the *Mary Celeste* in case no explosion or fire had destroyed the vessel. Probably a fresh northerly wind sprang up, filled the square sails and the vessel gathered way quickly. The peak halyard made fast at the usual place on the gaff would be brought at an acute angle around the stanchions at the gangway. With the heavy boat standing still at the end, I do not wonder that the halyard parted. This would tally exactly with the evidence given in court – that the peak halyard was broken.

The meteorological evidence also supports this theory. Surviving records of the Serviço Meteorologico dos Açores, the Portuguese authority covering the islands, attest that 'stormy conditions prevailed over the Azores on November 24 and 25'. However, those same records show that 'calm or light winds prevailed on the forenoon of the 25th'. The improvement did not last, however. In the afternoon a storm broke of almost unnatural ferocity. During the twenty-four-hour period, at Ponta Delgada, only fifty miles from where the disaster occurred, there was recorded a rainfall of 11·4 inches. The 'cold front' passed between three and eight p.m. Then the wind veered from south-west to north-west, which would have carried any small vessel not towards Santa Maria, but out into the Atlantic, where the nearest coast would be that of Portugal, eight hundred miles away.

There is recorded evidence that the alcohol *had* seeped from the *Mary Celeste*'s barrels. After the ship's eventual release from Admiralty custody in Gibraltar, she completed her voyage to Genoa, where it was discovered upon unloading that nine barrels were empty.

One person who never wavered in his belief that Captain Briggs and his family had been murdered was Gibraltar Attorney-General and Admiralty Proctor, Frederick Solly Flood. It was not until July 28, 1887 – fourteen years after he had had it made – that the analysis of the supposed blood upon the sword blade found in Captain Briggs's cabin was released, and then only because of pressure from the American State Department in Washington.

In the letter supplying him with the findings of Dr Patron, court registrar Edward Baumgartner wrote to the U.S. Consul on that date:

This analysis which was made by Dr Patron MD at the instance of Mr Solly Flood speaks for itself, it being rather remarkable, however, that the analysis or report so brought in, was brought in under seal on the 14th March, 1873, and the seal remained unbroken until I opened it for the purpose of giving you a copy.

The *Mary Celeste* continued to sail the oceans – although always with a crew – for twelve years after her mystery voyage.

Her ending was ignominious. The last registration entry in the records of the United States government – Number 28, issued on August 4, 1884 – is endorsed 'lost by stranding, January 3, 1885, on reefs off Rochelais, near Miragoane, Haiti. 7 on board. None lost.'

Kingman Putnam, a New York surveyor, discovered that a near-worthless cargo had been insured for $30,000 and that an insurance fraud had been planned between the master, Captain Gilman Parker and the U.S. Consul in Haiti. The consul fled into the jungle interior of Haiti and escaped arrest. Parker was arraigned on a charge of conspiracy and barratry, the wilful wrecking of a vessel, the penalty for which was death. There was a failure to agree at his first trial. He died before he could be brought before a second court.

It was two years after that – in July 1887 – that Consul Sprague responded to the American government's pressure about the blood sample and wrote in his letter to Washington:

This case of the Mary Celeste is startling, since it appears to be one of those mysteries which no human ingenuity can penetrate sufficiently to account for the abandonment of this vessel and the disappearance of her master, family and crew about which nothing has ever transpired.

Consul Sprague could have been mistaken.

On May 16, 1873, the Liverpool *Daily Albion* reported:
A sad story of the sea—a telegram from Madrid says 'Some fishermen at Baudus, in Asturias, have found two rafts, the first with a corpse lashed to it and an Agrican [American?] flag flying and the second raft with five decomposed bodies. It is not known to what vessel they belonged.'

It was never established nor even investigated if they might have been those of the people who disappeared from the *Mary Celeste*.